THE JEWELLER

THE JEWELLER

by Caryl Lewis

Translated from the Welsh
by Gwen Davies

HONNO MODERN FICTION

First published in the Welsh language in 2007 by Y Lolfa
First published in the English language in 2018 by Honno Press
'Ailsa Craig', Heol y Cawl, Dinas Powys, Vale of Glamorgan,
Wales, CF64 4AH
1 2 3 4 5 6 7 8 9 10

A catalogue record for this book is available from the British Library.
Published with the financial support of the Welsh Books Council.

ISBN 978-1-912905-05-8 (paperback)
ISBN 978-1-912905-06-5 (ebook)
Cover illustration © Teresa Jenellen
Cover design: Kari Brownlie
Text design: Elaine Sharples
Printed in Great Britain by 4edge Limited

I Mam, gyda diolch (CL)

Er cof am Gareth Alban Davies (GD)

Acknowledgements

Chapter 3 was first published in *New Welsh Review*. Special thanks to Suzy Ceulan Hughes and Mary-Ann Constantine, and to my family for advice and practical help, Sioned Rowlands of the Welsh Literature Exchange, Sally Baker and all at Translators' House Wales and Tŷ Newydd, Gioia and Ada at the Mrs Carter Italian translation workshop, Kathryn Gray and, above all, Caryl Lewis.

Gwen Davies, Translator

Ah! Happy they whose hearts can break
And peace of pardon win!...
... "How else but through a broken heart
May Lord Christ enter in?"
    Poem V, *The Ballad of Reading Gaol,* Oscar Wilde

Now when Jesus was risen early the first day of the week,
he appeared first to Mary Magdalene, out of whom he had
cast seven devils.
    Mark 16:9

Chapter 1

"In the name of the Father, the Son and the Holy..."

Mari opened her eyes. Down on her knees, she saw shapes forming in the dark. There came that fluttering sound again. At the little window, day was close; the wind's thin breath a cloud on the glass. A flutter, like fingers leafing through pages. She got up to look. Against the cold glass, a butterfly beat a muted prayer for escape. Her pupils got darker, helping her penetrate the grey. When she was a little girl they'd say butterflies were just leaves reincarnated. She'd mulled it over then, her mood lifted on a fancy of fortunes befalling a girl in a world where one small leaf can bloom all colours, sprout wings, up sticks and up up away into the sunset. She shivered.

The noise had awoken Nanw, who stretched out lazily. Mari went over and chattered to her softly to keep her calm. The sea was breathing in the distance, dark against the growing light, and seagulls were being flung across the air like litter. The butterfly nagged gently like an old flame. Should she let it outside, it was sure to die, weak and failing as it already was from a winter in the cottage. But it was desperate to be let go. Nanw sat up, enchanted by the ragged wings. Mari caught it at the corner of the glass, cupping her hands around it as though she were receiving communion. She nudged open the sash with her elbow, the wings pulsing weakly on her palm. She stretched her arms out and a gust snatched the insect away across the garden. Now you could hear the ringing of wind in the rigging of boats below. Fear crept through her. She banged the window shut and drew the loose folds of her nightie around her. She gazed into the gloom, the butterfly's powder a gold dust on her fingertips.

"Amen," she whispered.

Nanw was mimicking her by leaning against her cage's grid, arms clutched round her body. The weak light glowed silver in Mari's hair, and ruby across the dark face of the monkey.

The chill had crept up Mari's spine so she fetched a cardigan and hooked it over her shoulders. She let the cat into the bedroom to keep Nanw company while she had her breakfast.

The cottage was nestled on a remote road above the sea, surrounded by crooked trees. Opposite the low doorway, across the road, was an old stile marking the way down to the beach. The three small rooms were filled with clutter. Mari's treasures choked the narrow kitchen passage, and vintage clothes hung along each wall. Papers were piled all anyhow, while the thick walls were so badly affected by damp that she had to keep a fire going in the bedroom. She went barefoot along the lino to the kitchen and lowered an egg on a spoon into a saucepan of water. She dried the spoon on her nightie, thrusting it into some cranny of an old wireless needing technical TLC after Nanw broke the aerial in a fit of temper. Mari listened to the radio's far-off voices as she made herself a cup of tea. She left the teabag steaming on the sink.

She waited for the egg to rap out in Morse code that it was ready, and she sat down to eat at that early hour. Mari finished her egg, leaving the shell rocking on the table.

In the bedroom she put on two pairs of socks, and pushed her petticoat into the top of her trousers. Tying her money bag around her waist, she hid it under rolls of jumper. She threw some nuts over to Nanw who set to cracking them, eager for the next one even before she'd had the first. Years ago, the monkey would have gone with her mistress: she had been good for business. But times had changed; one nip and a customer would play hell. Mari crouched to say goodbye, stroking her little black hands, while Nanw tried to filch the bracelets chiming around Mari's wrists. The cat half-woke and whipped her tail in envy.

"Stay here now, sweetie; the cat'll keep you company."

Mari stood up, letting go of the hands which curled back around the bars. Nanw turned her big eyes on her. Mari shut the door and went into the front room. She rummaged among the teddies in the toy chest and found a deep leather box. She held it tight against her breast like a child and carried it out carefully to the car, locking the door behind her.

Squalls stifled the sound of the engine starting up. The clock's staccato said quarter to five. Dry leaves and rubbish were being blown about the garden. From her cell, Nanw saw the car depart, and she glanced out into the garden at a small colourful leaf clutching at blades of grass. The cat began to purr.

Chapter 2

The market had a real buzz about it, with boxes being hauled up high on shoulders. Wednesday, the traditional mart day, was busiest. Even though the animal auction in town had closed years ago, a dwindling number of local farm wives still kept to custom. Most of the stallholders had already unpacked, priced and displayed their goods and were tucking into bacon sandwiches from Ann Chips' café where she thrust them at you with big arms marked with a grid of pink scars like streaks in bacon.

As the sun shone higher through the old hall's roof, so the chatter rose in volume. This time of year, the place looked pretty worn out. Neon starburst signs insisted you appreciate their advertised bargains, while the unforgiving spring light flooded over well-thumbed stock. Even the voices of the marketeers as they fell out – shouting – sounded gravelly, in need of a good sluicing.

Mari greeted everyone shyly as she picked her way towards her stall, feeling herself relax as she melted into the comforting din. Fish and meat smells mixed with fag smoke and steam from teacups, a scent so strong it phased out trespassing thoughts. She fumbled for her keys, noticing Dafydd had kindly opened the heavy doors of her stall already. Next to hers, Gwyn had his already open. They nodded to each other. He was a cobbler: his shoes, stuffed with raffle tickets, were set out shipshape on shelves. He cut keys too, and with a timely tink of his screwdriver would set running again the odd dawdling watch. On her other side,

Mo was selling some woman a dishcloth and Lifebuoy soap. She twirled the carrier bag around her wrist and knotted it. When she wrinkled her nose behind her no-frills glasses, the window between her teeth seemed to widen. She winked at Mari, and she smiled back like she always did.

It was getting crowded. Some customers came every day just to fetch meat or bread: they dipped like kingfishers into the maelstrom and flitted off, meal in beak. Others called in on their way to shop in town, to get a key cut or a shoe mended, to buy jam or browse for a gift. Some even came especially to look at the dolls' house on Gwyn's stall: someone's home in perfect detail, down to the last fingernail shoehorn. Today he had Easter eggs in a row of cups along the four-inch kitchen table. Iwan was the type of customer who would stay there all day since retiring. He came by bus and leaned on counters chatting till they kicked him out at hometime. In the café he'd join anyone who was sitting on their own. He gave Mari a grin but had his sights set on Mo.

"Well, Mo, lookin' fine, lookin' swell..." A cocked eyebrow in Mari's direction.

"What's that supposed to mean then, Iwan?"

"Looking... 'well-upholstered', shall we say?"

Mo put her hand on her stomach.

"For your information, Iwan love, I'm like a rake under all these clothes... May look like a bag lady in this get-up but at least it keeps the draughts out." Iwan laughed. One of the girls from the baker's smiled as she passed. "Now put me down or Dai'll be wanting words with you."

"That old pussycat?"

"Well now, Iwan love, what you want then?" They began ferreting in a box of socks.

Mari's stall was long and narrow, with glass cases in front and shelves behind to display the bigger items and vintage clothing. Just looking at the leather box spread a warm feeling through her veins. This was her favourite time of day. Like opening a beehive, she pulled out the velvet trays from its belly and let the jewels flood out their own light. The glass necklaces and the cameos with their milky faces stayed at the market, locked up overnight. But the valuable stones would come and go as she did. Each morning she would wake them, spread them out under a glass altar, waiting for them to lure their worshippers.

She let the gems come alive and germinate: diamond and emerald, bloodstone and ruby. Their beauty was something she never came to terms with. All the earth's power had gone into forming something this stunning. Sometimes in a deep seam of her dreams, rocks were locked in a cosmic duel, their sweat dripping off as jewels. She had black pearls from some exotic lakes, too: little globes with a sheen across them in the gentle light. When a stone had been well cut, you didn't need bright electric lamps to show it off.

Mari took out a huge sapphire ring which she had just bought at an auction. She rubbed it with an old rag to warm it up. Its blue-green was deceptively deep like the sea; she could see fleets out there, sunk in its watery hall of mirrors.

"New, is it?"

She jumped. Iwan liked to keep an eye on her stock and would buy a watch at the market now and then, even though he didn't have many appointments to attend. She showed him the ring and he held it awkwardly.

"Sapphire," she said, "the stone of wisdom."

"Well, well..."

She leaned over the counter, happy to see him absorbed in blue depths.

"They used to think the world was set in a huge sapphire and that's why the sky is blue."

"Pretty," he said, giving it back, "but a bit out of my league."

"But you'd be the wisest man here, then… All the answers to the world's big questions in there, you know."

"Well," he said, tapping his temple, "my noggin's nearly hollow, but I'd rather stay a numbskull if being clever costs that much!"

He laughed and pushed his new socks into his suit pocket, limping over to the café. Mari rubbed the sapphire again, considering it a reasonable price for all the world's answers. She placed it in among the other pieces which cast a prism of colour across the faces of passers-by.

Chapter 3

"We'd better kneel down then," Mari said.

Mo grumbled as she sought some clear space in the middle of the floor. You could see the shape of her horseshoe brooch through her jumper. It was Maundy Thursday and Mo had fetched Mari to help her, as her husband was at auction. Mo sold knickers, bloomers, vests and aprons by day. She'd tried lately to keep up with the fashion by stocking the occasional tiger-print bra or snaking a purple feather boa around the flannelette and Y-fronts. But it was by night she made her money. She did "nest clearance" as she put it: pecking like a magpie over the pickings of empty old houses, clearing them and sorting out their relics into piles for sale or burning. Every week she'd sift through old lives and tidy them away into black bags and auction lots. Mari often went along to keep Mo company, and, in return, she got first refusal on clothes and jewellery.

Tonight, the women were in a house high above the harbour. Below them, seagulls strutted with sour faces through the empty harbour's black shale. The rain was slapping testily at the windows of the old Georgian residence.

Hands clasped, the pair prayed on the carpet in the dark until their knees ached.

"Watch out, now."

There being no electricity, Mo got up and lit a lamp. She pulled Mari to her feet.

Every nook of the cavernous living room was crammed, with just a sheep's track picking its way through. It stank too;

when it had got too much to bear, Mari had muffled her mouth in her scarf. Dozens of empty sugar packets were in one corner; in another, carrier bags of milk bottles.

The light flashed in owl eyes, their owner perched in a cabinet by the fireplace. Mari felt coldness clutching. Mo marked its case with a chalk cross, a system for her husband to see which items to collect for auction. She marked a corner cupboard in the same way. Mari got out her torch and switched it on. She heard rustling from the chimney: probably a bird nesting up there. On the mantelpiece were black and white photographs. A girl riding a bike, hair done up in a Marcel Wave and ribbon. Her check blouse was knotted at the waist, and her long legs were working the pedals to speed her past happily while she looked back laughing. A soldier. A wedding photo. The same woman on the beach in middle age. Another of her, sixty, on her birthday. She hadn't had time to have children. That was why it had been left to strangers such as her and Mo to comb through her life.

She felt some affinity with this girl and ran a finger over the sepia. An old longing awoke in Mari and so, once Mo's back was turned, she shoved the picture into her pocket. She smoothed the flap down and switched off her torch.

"Poor old thing," Mo muttered, "kept everything!" She put out the lamp. "Come on."

The pair went upstairs in the dark, pausing now and then to let Mo cough up some of the smoker's tar pooling in the pit of her lungs for the past fifty years. There were telltale squares of darker wallpaper where a sly neighbour must have called to steal the more valuable pictures.

"Didn't Dafydd say he was coming to help?" Mo gasped.

"Must be busy," Mari shrugged.

"Oh-h," Mo groaned, moving her weight onto one knee

10

and pulling herself up by the banister. As they climbed higher, a little sun filtered through the skylight. Mo lit the lamp in the big bedroom while Mari went into the smaller one and opened the curtains. A nightdress was still on the bed and the blankets had been thrown back.

The old woman must have slept in this bed, not in the double. Mari snooped through the dressing table. The guilt of rummaging around in someone's things never eased, even though she'd been at it for years. She riffled through the old tights and hankies. The bottom drawer was laid with white tablecloths – for best – with an ivy border, expensive blankets and hand-embroidered aprons. They hadn't ever been used: there'd clearly been no occasion which counted as special enough. A yellowing packet of confetti, button-up gloves and a lace collar. Mari carefully opened a shoebox, listening to Mo's chalk scratching next door. Wartime love letters on official notepaper, a diamond dress ring, a blue brooch and a string of pearls. Nothing especially interesting. She restored the room to order and drew one blanket back over the bed. A glass of water was still at the bedside, bubbles sticking stubbornly to its base.

She opened the wardrobe, keeping her palm flat on the wood. Frocks, suits. A long fur coat. She pulled it out slightly into the light. It seemed brand new, the healthy fur shining.

"My God!" Mo cried. Mari jumped and swung the mirror to. Mo had money: a fistful of notes. "Serious cash in here!" Mo showed her a coat with its sleeves sewn shut; she shoved the money into her pocket. "Don't give me that look. Nobody knows it's here and the grandkids are always on about wanting something or another. Just a nice little bonus, this is."

"Asking for bad luck, you are," Mari warned.

"Don't get much good luck anyway." Mo took the lamp with her out of the room.

Mari was looking at the lumpy bed with its blanket pulled tight. She knew it happened all the time. She herself had bought jewellery from a man, not knowing he was an undertaker who had prised it from the body. When she'd challenged him later, his excuse was, "No use for jewels underground!" But he was clearly ignorant of where they came from in the first place.

They always finished up in the kitchen with a ritual of tea from Mo's flask, and biscuits. It was old fashioned and even darker here. The lamp caught the glass of a clock in the corner which had slowed in its tracks and stopped. Mo crossed it with chalk and checked it over. Mari switched on her torch and the pair gasped. The remains of supper were still on the table, dirty cutlery and all. The food had gone rotten black. Mo tidied a knife and fork onto a plate as they should be placed after a meal.

"The last supper," Mari said, smiling sadly.

When they were in the porch getting ready to go out into the rain, Mo stuffed the notes back into the folds of a coat hanging up there. The door shut fast behind them. At the harbourside, lulled by a lapping tide, the women walked through the rain. Mari rubbed the picture, crisp in her pocket.

Chapter 4

On Good Friday, Mari was struggling with the stall doors. Tiredness leached through her body – especially her arms – after her work the previous night. She hoped someone might help, but Gwyn hadn't arrived yet and Mo was in full flow over at the bakery. Mari flushed at the idea of asking a stranger. Two young women walked past. She tried to make the doors give way, tugging sharply, and started to sweat. Lately the weakness settled on her like sea mist, taking all morning to lift. She made sure no one had noticed her. She was about to give up. Resting her head against the doors, her face was red with strain. Every day she felt fatigue shake her harder like a rag doll, and yet her nerves were on edge.

"Mari?" Dafydd's quiet voice.

His white coat was all bloody from chopping up meat; the knife he was holding was wet. Mari stepped aside and let him solve her problem with one hand. She tried not to catch his eye in case he saw how close she was to tears.

"Thanks," she cleared her throat. She hurried to open the inner door just as Dafydd bent to pick up her box. Their heads nearly touched.

"Watch out, or you'll get blood on it," she said, taking it from him and setting it on the counter.

"Missed me?"

Mari was ferreting in the box. "No."

He got a bag of flesh out of his pocket.

"Look, these are for Nanw."

"Bring them over later."

Dafydd sighed.

"I can't come tonight, but don't forget to give them to her."

Mari slipped out the jewellery trays as usual. The gems were sparkling, humming like bees, their corners pricking her fingers.

"Well, can't be helped," she said.

"But I'll come over soon."

"That's enough porkies."

"Mari..."

She smiled.

They heard a man's polite cough. Dafydd stepped back and hovered nearby. It was a couple entwined, his hands caked with black. Her young skin seemed polished, and at her hairline there was blonde down. The middle-aged man squeezed her arm until white bands appeared around it. Dafydd looked them up and down.

"Time to choose, then," the man said. The girl's eyes flitted from ring to ring, no idea where to start. "I'll pay cash," he added.

"We've just got engaged," she said as if in apology. Mari dipped her head, still setting out her wares. One thing a ring can do is hold you to a promise. But that sort of promise was far too heavy for this girl's slight shoulders. After years of being longed for, loved and flaunted by other owners, the jewels shared Mari's company a while before finding a new home. She expected one of them to choose this girl. Competing for her favour, their angles ogled: the gems shone keenly, mean. Dafydd was watching the girl eye the polished facets.

"This one, I think," she said at last. A diamond ring whose impressive dazzle made up for its size.

"Will you wear it now?"

The girl glanced at her fiancé. "Hm, I might lose it."

"What's the point of buying it then? You got it, baby, you should flaunt it!"

He put down his money on the counter while Mari wrote out a receipt and rooted around for a box. She could tell he was not used to waiting, so she took her time. Dafydd was shuffling from one foot to the other.

"Do you know why a diamond sparkles?" Mari held captive her audience of three. The girl slipped the ring on, slipped the ring off. "It's because any light that gets in splits into a prism." Dafydd had taken a step closer. "It bounces off walls in there, dances; it catches fire." The girl was half-smiling as she gawked at her finger. "It's like a house for the jewel. But if those walls aren't smooth, or if that home isn't ready and there's no welcome, then... that gem will break its heart and hide away that flicker. The light is lost..." The girl's expression clouded. Mari scored the receipt into a fold with her nail and gave it to the man. He plucked it from her with a frown. "Congratulations!"

The girl twisted around as the man tried to tug her away. Mari did not blanch at the dark look Dafydd gave her.

Chapter 5

Mari was sitting at the lip of the bed, the carrier bag in her lap and her mind light years away. It was evening, the night clouds coming in to colour the sky. She couldn't keep her eyes off that photo of the bicycling girl, which she'd framed and placed on the mantelpiece along with the others. The girl seemed at home there, somehow: among friendly souls. Nanw's screech cut across the room. Mari chose another piece of meat. The monkey snatched it, swallowed most of it whole, squealing and groping between the bars for more. On her way home from work – passing the town square – Mari had seen Dafydd walking hand in hand with a slender, dark-haired girl. Making sure they didn't see her, Mari had stood there until the cold settled around her.

"Damn you!" She dropped the bag and stood up. Mad for the meat, Nanw had given her a nip. "Little devil! What d'you do that for?" Nanw laughed spitefully in response. "You stroppy so-and-so!" Two puncture points on her finger pricked red. "Well, damn you, then! You hear?"

In the kitchen, Mari turned on the tap, watching the water run pink. Feeling the cut sting, she bandaged it in a tea towel. Back she went along the passage hung with party frocks, trying to calm down. The day was creeping from them but it cast a late light across the lace frocks whose froth was all around her. Nanw still had her eye on the bag, while the cat was helping herself to its contents and baiting the monkey whenever she got too close. Mari did not leave until she felt bile rising in her throat.

In the best room, Mari sat on Nanw's toy box. Here, the fireplace had been blocked up, while stacked across the floor were cartons of paperwork. In the alcove was her work desk where she restrung pearls or repaired brooches. She had a wheel for cutting stones and, on the wall-shelf, rows of bottles containing chemicals and polishing powders. It was time to put the jewels away, so she took them off the desk and tucked them up to sleep in their little velvet beds. Locking the double padlock for night-time security, she mulled over the sales she'd made. A ring she'd never liked. That silly girl: fancy going for the flashiest ring available! That couple certainly wasn't set for a happy future. But serve her right if she would choose a charmer. Mari bent back into the box in pursuit of some rough material. Out it came, wrapped around something heavy. Blood was showing through her bandage but the old white cloth was already dirty. The last of the sunrays were arrowing their way inside. Nanw was still whining away.

She took out a treasure and examined it inch by inch. Dense and solid, it made Mari's body tense. It was a stone of raw emerald: a rough face which revealed its true colours in the half-light. These were hues of harsh spring green that turned the sunset's yellow into a sickly mix. She hadn't touched it for years, but as she held it up to the window, she could almost see it winking at her like a kindred spirit.

She'd been a child when it had enthralled her from its showcase in an antique shop. Her father would call on his parishioners in town, leaving her free to wander the streets. To the owner working inside, Mari's face was a regular envious smudge against his shop window, although she pretended she was only interested in his craftsmanship. She went there so often that he eventually offered her a Saturday job. She worked there years for a pittance just to save up for the jewel. She had promised herself that its first incision would be made with herself at the wheel. She marvelled how such a coarse veil could conceal the face of a goddess. She'd tricked her father into thinking she was working at the baker's, guessing he'd disown her should he see how impressed she was by worldly gewgaws. But we shouldn't be afraid of beauty, should we?

Since possessing the stone, Mari had struggled to admire it without wanting to cut it. To open in it just the smallest window. But yes, of course such gorgeous uncut gems can trick you. She'd heard of jewellers sent insane by years of knowing a stone's face as incisively as they did their own. They'd put all their faith in it. Been led to believe they had the key to every cell. That it was rock solid. But they'd take up their tools and it would flake to powder just the same. Leaving the memory of that germ of beauty.

Just imagine. Once more Mari hid the gem's face in its dirty rag. Down it went among the playthings. As it sank from view, she felt herself revive. She slammed the lid closed and searched along the mantelpiece for the old Bible. As heavy as a gravestone, with a fading golden crucifix on its cover, it served to stop the box's secrets rising. She took a deep breath.

Settled at her desk, she drew a pile of old photos and letters into her lap. Nanw was in a mood, but Mari ignored the noise and read until dusk neared. She lit a lamp and the cat slunk in, leaping lightly onto her despite a bellyful of meat. Oh, how her bones ached! But these mementoes revived Mari. She warmed her hands by their fire. The world slipped from day's clasp. The emerald stayed warm in its swaddling: like a piece of coal, its grey face was impassive, hiding the green fuse driving within it.

Chapter 6

All Saturday morning, Mo had been trying to coax Mari out of her shell. Both had shut up their stalls early as the plan was for Mo's husband Dai to take them in his van to clean out a church later on. Dai and his mate would remove all the pews the next day, but Mari and Mo's job was to lift the mats, box the Bibles, clear the vestry and move what was left into the porch – anything, at any rate, that would fit into the van.

Hundreds of swallows were arriving each day now, some high-tailing it in the clear blue sky, some threading the telegraph wires where they'd shake their feathers as though to shed winter itself. Mari was sitting between Mo and Dai in a fug of nicotine. Dai noticed the plaster on Mari's finger.

"That bloody monkey again?"

Mari shook her head. Mo let a slice of air into the cab.

"No. Me being clumsy cutting a stone," Mari said, folding her fingers into her fist.

Mo's eyebrow went up, one corner of her mouth down, as she blew out her smoke sideways.

"Here we are!" Dai said as he squeezed down a narrow lane and stopped. A For Sale sign loomed at them from among bare branches.

"Be back for you later."

Mo picked up a basket of their usual provisions from the cab and blew her husband a kiss before he drove off.

"OK?" Mo asked. She took out black bags, giving them to Mari to carry.

The old church, with its Sunday-school house, was set at

the end of a track. The whitewash bloomed green, while weeds had set up home in the cracks and were creeping every which way across the walls. Mo opened a gate and Mari picked out her way behind her. The track wound through yews which turned blue sky dark green. Mo pulled her scarf tighter and fumbled for the key. The door had swollen in the recent rain; the women had to pitch their weight against it, their efforts steaming white against the still air. Mo was coughing.

Mo left the door wide open and tried the switch inside. It had rusted, streaming orange down the cream paint. They both looked heavenwards but there was no light. The church was tiny: only six small, narrow casements, an organ loft and a simple stained-glass altar window of the Crucifixion. A shame the chalice and patens had been stolen. The damp had stamped its watermark of grey roses on the altar cloth.

Mari got out a pair of gloves, prising open the black sack's stubborn lips, a prayer on her own. The women worked for hours. The red carpet was lifted from the floor and packed into a neat roll. Their loot of prayer cushions made a large pile by the door. The numbers to call hymns were on cards kept in their own little case: Mari counted each one out and put them carefully back in place. Mo had her eye on the organ and marked it, giving her companion a smile. Mari took off her gloves in order to carry six vases, one from each sill; the smelly water she sluiced away at the outside tap. They realised it was warmer outside than in, so Mo brought out two stools. Mari went back into the chilly church to fetch and fold the altar cloth so she could take it home to wash before returning it to Mo.

Draping the cloth over her arm, Mari gently pinched the material between her fingers. She'd had the chance once, when she was a child, to be an altar server. For months she'd marked how the other children did it, following the rote. Her important day arrived. She had worn the white gown, goggled at herself mirrored in the brass cross. The perfect cherub, bursting to please, for it all to be just so. So much so that her nerves had snapped, and she'd let the communion wine spill across her dress. She closed her eyes, hearing again around the church walls the aching echo of that cup's landing. She'd cried in front of the whole congregation as though it was blood on her dress, bloodshed on her hands. She'd stayed in the vestry, waiting for her father – weeping – until the service ended and he'd snatched her from there with a few sharp words. The dress had had to be burnt: the stain had run too deep.

"Mari?"

A sculpture of Jesus was nailed to the wall. Mari was studying the light wood, the drops of blood, the scrap of dark blue about his middle. Mo came over and stood behind her.

"What'll we do with it? It's in memory of someone." Mari's words blew out a warm mist.

Mo wrinkled up her nose, trying to read the plaque underneath. "Shame to leave him behind; he'll just get thrown out. I'll fetch a stool: we'll manage... Grab him by the loincloth!"

Off she bustled while in Mari there grew the sense of stained glass lending heat and power to the evening light. Mo returned with the stool and placed it under the sculpture. One of Mo's legs was stiff from the cold, so it was Mari who had to face the ascent.

She'd thought the stool had been steady when she'd climbed onto it, holding Mo's hand to give her faith. Mari reached out for the sculpture. But the stool started to rock on a loose slate.

"You won't fall," Mo told her, even though she couldn't see properly. Mari grabbed hold of Jesus' feet, but he wouldn't budge.

"It's stuck. I need something to bang it with."

"Wait," Mo replied, letting go of the stool suddenly so it shook again.

Mari heard her out in the vestry. Though the light was going fast outside, in here it was multiplied in multi-coloured lozenges. Mo's footsteps were amplified in the empty church. She was carrying a sizeable crucifix.

"Give him a bash with this!"

Mari jammed herself against the wall. She struck the sculpture's feet until paint peeled off in curlicues, a shower of shavings over Mari like Manna. Down below, Mo was coughing.

"Any good?"

"Nearly there..." A final bang. The screw had loosened from the damp plaster, making the sculpture sway slightly. Giving the cross back to Mo, Mari gripped the feet and pulled them. To the crack of crumbling plaster, the sculpture descended to Earth. For a small object, it was quite heavy; Mari tucked it under her arm as though it were a baby, taking Mo's other hand to help her jump down safely.

"He's cute, isn't he?" Mo said, screwing up her eyes to get a proper look. "Bound to find a good home somewhere."

By the time it had all been carried off into the porch, darkness had almost fallen. Mari searched for the Births and Deaths Register, but couldn't find it; it must have gone to another church in the parish. But she had collected a bundle of letters and records from the vestry and put it aside for herself.

Mo uncovered the basket, and the pair sat on the altar step. The damp walls were bejewelled with yellow and purple diamonds of light. The windows were washed with gilt, the ivy outside a dark fretwork in silhouette. Mari was mesmerised by the sight as Mo opened the flask, moaning that her friend wouldn't let her use the altar as their picnic table.

Mo spread the sandwiches and biscuits over the cold slates. The women crouched together, their reddish overcoats a drop of bright colour in the chill grey setting. They ate in silence, the tea's steam and their breath a sinuous streamer. Mo lit a post-snack cigarette, the tip a red spot in the darkness. She'd ignored Mari fretting about her smoking: the church was empty anyway.

"Hope Dai gets here soon," Mo's voice reverberated. Mari gave a little shrug. "Must have got held up somewhere." Mo glanced about, feeling small in the solemn atmosphere. "Think God'll put a curse on us then?"

"Don't be daft." Mari didn't sound convinced. "God wouldn't curse anyone!"

The women listened to the wind which was starting to whip the ivy against the glass.

"Well, put it like this, then," Mo said. "Don't reckon we'll be welcome in his home now we've shown how light our fingers are!"

She laughed chestily, taking a drag. But Mari had caught a flash of something in the dark: Jesus' pearly flesh shining in the church porch.

Chapter 7

Late the following evening, the altar cloth was hanging up to dry. The flames lit up a frown in gold and silver threads across the cloth's smooth brow. The papers she'd taken from the church were strewn across the bed. Mari's eyes were bloodshot. Guilt had plagued her till she'd stopped thinking about the cross and sculpture as stolen treasures. After all, better with Mo than local thieves. Nanw was sulking: Mari was on the hunt again.

She couldn't find what she wanted, though, so Mari put the papers aside. The monkey's fingers were plying the bars of her little prison. Mari peered under the bed. She brought out an ebony-lidded box. Nanw's head was cocked into a question mark, her eyes following her mistress' every move as her hands worried the grain of its lid. The heat steamed the stink of the damp church out of the cloth. Mari frowned then opened the box. Hidden away there were black and white photos of her as a baby and a little girl. Her father smiling for the camera; her first day at school; Mari standing in the garden as a schoolgirl with a rosebush for company; father and daughter having a fun day at the seaside. Even though it made her nauseous, she allowed herself the ache of looking at the place beside her father. It was taken up by empty space.

The moon's face was gone a moment; Mari's head jerked up. Nanw too was listening. Letting the pictures fall askew across the floor, Mari kicked them and the box back under the bed. She stood against the door so no one could see her from outside. Nanw giggled. The fire in the chimney drew, sucking at the papers on the bed. Burglars were a continual threat: after all, anyone could follow her and her precious cargo home from the market. Mo came with her to her car but anyone could break into the cottage.

Footsteps. No! She hadn't locked her jewellery up properly. Best thing was to play for time, hide the key to that room. The idea of losing the emerald... Bare feet sticking to the lino, she opened the door. The passage was silent, but there was definitely someone there. Someone who was trying the door knob.

Bang, bang, bang...

A fist hammering. Her body started to give, like paper in water.

Bang, bang, bang...

She must just stay still.

"Mari! Let me in." Her legs were almost pulp. But the voice was familiar. "Mari, open the door!"

She curled a fist at her belly to force herself upright. Sliding open the bolts, she opened up. Dafydd was leaning against the doorframe, his face half black with blood.

"I knew this would happen!" she cried out. He slumped forward and lunged towards her, his body pressing an imprint of blood and dirt onto her nightie. His shirt was wet. Mari hoisted him awkwardly from under his armpits and dragged him over to her bedroom. She swatted the papers from the bed and let him down gently to sitting. Nanw was bickering with herself, reaching out manically through the bars for the meat-treats she was expecting from the butcher.

"Shush!" Mari scolded. Dafydd was lolling forward like a seed head giving up on its stalk.

"Stay here," she patted his arm then went to fetch hot water and a cloth. She sat in a chair facing him, a bowl in her lap. He was swiping at his tears with the back of his hand. His hands were unmarked, at any rate. His chin in her hands, he

28

stared far off into the night. Mari dabbed away quietly, letting the wet drip back into the bowl, bringing the bloom of blood to the water's clarity. They tried to close their ears to Nanw's continuous complaint.

"They're going to shut the market." Dafydd avoided addressing her directly. She evaded answering him but caught his eye, went back to washing. "D'you hear? They're going to close it."

Nanw was whooping hysterically.

"Don't be silly."

"They don't want us any more, Mana..."

He hadn't called her that since his boyhood. His forehead was scalding. She was surprised how coarse his skin was under her fingertips; she hadn't touched his face since he'd started shaving.

"Mam went over the club tonight..."

"Came home to the bottle, did she?"

"She's afraid we'll lose Dat's business."

"I knew she was at it again."

"Don't want everyone..."

"I'm not everyone, Dafydd. She's not fit..."

"She doesn't know what she's doing..." His voice cracked.

She straightened his chin so he had to make eye contact. You could almost see her bones through the skin on her hands. "She knows full well! Just look at your lovely face..."

"Don't!" He tucked his chin into his neck.

"Look at your face." She ran her fingers over his cheekbones, wondering whether the scars would mark him for life. Wet blood smeared his forehead. "The spit of your father." Mari was miles away and close to tears.

Dafydd's hold on her wrist pinched like a cheap bracelet. Mari stopped her work. They looked deep into each other's eyes.

"Please don't," he said. "Please..."

Mari knelt before him.

"Get away from here, love, far away. Make a new life for yourself somewhere else. She'll tear you to pieces..."

"But I've got a girlfriend... We're – you know – Catrin and me are getting married."

She felt his emotions puffing onto her cheek.

"You're too young. This is stupid. I've told you before!"

"But we're..."

"Quiet!" Mari wrung out the cloth and got up like an old woman. "There we are: all clean now."

"Mana... we're going to lose the business. We'll all have to... I don't know..."

By moonlight she poured the dirty water down the kitchen sink. By the time she returned, his head had sunk lower and his cheek had started to swell. He was staring at the corner of the box under the bed. She could hardly breathe.

"What's that?" he asked in a low voice.

"Nothing," she whispered back.

"Box."

"Shhhhhh."

"What's in it?"

"You're tired... Lie down a minute." His eyes were starting to close. "Come on now, you just lie here for a little rest."

She knelt to undo his laces. He took off his own shirt and lay down. He was asleep in an instant. She relaxed and leaned her head against the bedstead. Nanw, copying the rise and fall of Dafydd's chest, was curled up asleep at the base of her cage like a heavy hank of hair cut from the scalp.

The fire burnt low, only brighter now and then as the wind's bellows worked in the chimney. Mari picked up his bloody shirt – his body's warmth fleeing her fingers – and folded it over the bedpost. Her shadow shaded him as she leaned over to push the box right back under the bed.

His shoulders were square and solid, his muscles had filled out. Dafydd had changed so much since he was a little boy. Twenty-one years old in a few months' time! Years ago he'd scream out in his sleep, startling Nanw. He wouldn't have said boo to a goose at that age. His mother wasn't fit to care for him.

His skin was slightly flushed, his torso white and soft. How on earth could he sleep all exposed like that? Mari always slept with an arm across her chest protecting her throat. The clouds above the sea moved away from the moon, rippling silver shadows over his muscles. His skin looked warm, smooth: a drumskin tight across his Adam's apple. Cramped up in her chair by the bed, she gazed at the crooked scars on his face and body. How she loved this lad.

When Mari woke first thing in her chair, the bed was empty, only Dafydd's shape left on the eiderdown and envelopes crinkled flat where she'd left them last night. She hadn't slept so soundly for years. As she stirred, so did Nanw. Mari opened the cage and pulled the sleepy monkey onto her lap. Nanw's tail looped itself around her guardian and Mari nursed her, cheek to cheek, feeling some warmth seep into the cold little hands.

Chapter 8

Mari had gone back to bed with Nanw knotted around one arm. It was Easter Sunday and both of them had slept through the afternoon. She sat up, disengaging monkey limbs from her own. She got dressed in silence, skipping prayers, all the time an eye on that small body on her single bed. Tiptoeing, Mari left the room. The birds in the trees around the cottage were serenading the departing day; she stood on the threshold inhaling deeply. She crossed the road and climbed carefully over the narrow stile.

It was a crisp evening, even though the wind had died down. The path descended steeply towards the sea, cutting through richer pasture. The sheep were sheltering under walls, flowers shrugged themselves lower into grass. Mari shoved her hands deep into her pocket. She so loved the racket of the market. Could she stand the quiet life, no stake at all in the thick of things? Really it was a lifeline for Iwan, giving him an excuse for an expedition. She thought about Dafydd's stall, the butcher's.

The low tide had peeled off a mile-long paring of soft sand all along the coastline. The bay here was shallow; the forking headlands encrusted with big black stacks. The currents called a truce around these rocks. Today one of them offered succour to a cormorant in widower's weeds, searching for his love in vain across the waves. The air was cool. Mari kept as close to the dunes and as far from the sea as possible. A distant beachcomber was knee-deep among seaweed and driftwood, coughed up at the tidemark. She scanned the shore for a flat stone to sit on. The tide had dragged the sea from its prey this time but the sea's scraping talons showed the day's battle all down the sand. Mermaid's purses lay shattered at her feet.

Mari would come here when she needed time to think. Sometimes she even prayed into the sea breeze. The painstaking figure came closer, paused and peered towards her. She gave him a small smile and Gwyn came up and sat on a boulder beside her.

Although they had worked side by side for years, they hardly ever talked to one another. Mari used to bring him a morning mug of tea and pick his brains about the intricacies of clockmaking. But he wasn't one to waste words, and each encounter with the slight man seemed to leave him further away from her than ever. So embarrassing was it for them both by the end that they'd settled instead on a speechless exchange of views.

"Have you heard, then?" he whispered. She nodded. Birds were whirling over the waves. His voice seemed displaced outdoors, outside work's noise. "It was bound to happen. All towns'll be the same soon." He had a sack across his back which he now swung onto the sand. He looked different too, purple jumper draining eyes to watery blue. "Mo'll be all right, I suppose," he paused, "and you?"

The sea kept on sieving pebbles.

"Don't know." She listened to the pull and push of water. "I can't afford a shop in town." Heaven help her if she had to get a proper job. And all the other market towns were much too far away.

"They'll make a fuss, I s'pose: posters, petition and that, but..."

"Bet they've already made their minds up," Mari finished his sentence. Gwyn kept flicking his wedding ring with his thumbnail. How could she get up at all with no market to go out to, Mari wondered? "And what will you do?" she asked.

"Well, I'm too old for anything much now." His expression was playful. "Always thought maybe I should get away. See the world." A pause. "But maybe I've left that too late, too."

"You're not too old… What about your wife?" She hesitated.

His voice was faint, like the sea in a seashell far from shore. "I'm… I'm sure she wouldn't mind."

"You're lucky," Mari said. Gwyn was startled. "Lucky you've got…" She stopped and he got up. "All I've got is past lives." She ventured further. "All those people and all those houses." She picked up an empty mussel shell. "I don't think they ever go for good, you know? I don't think they get lost."

They were both mulling over Mari's words. Had she gone too far, Mari worried?

"Well, I don't believe there are ghosts stalking the earth, but I do think they find a place to live in someone else's life," Gwyn offered.

Mari felt her heart racing. "That's just what I think!" She gave him a shy grin. "Sometimes I've got so many pressing down on me it's a miracle I don't get suffocated."

Gwyn laughed sadly. Quiet thickened between them, thinned only by the sound of the sea. He thumbed his ring in the dark. The cries of the seagulls were harsh.

Pins and needles were stabbing her backside. A delicate mist – a lace hemming – had hidden the horizon and, wraithlike, was making its way up the beach. Her guts pounded along with the waves; her thoughts were wispy, like a wedding veil.

"Mari? Are you all right?"

It felt as though seawater were sloshing through her limbs. "A bit funny, that's all."

35

"Come on, I'll walk you back home."

Shouldering his sack, Gwyn helped her up. The wheeling of the birds, the way the waves were clawing the gravel, were making her feel sick. She could hear the submerged grains of grit scratching the rough of stones away: annihilating the marks that make each one unique.

When they reached the stile, Gwyn helped her get over it. Then he turned towards the harbour and the town.

"Did you find it?" she shouted after him. He faltered. "Did you find it? What you were looking for just now on the beach?"

He shook his head with a sliver of a smile. "I don't know. Things'll come out in the wash, Mari. Things'll get better, you'll see."

When Mari closed the door last thing, the draught huffed halves of swallow eggshells across the floor. The little cups looked like the remnants of an elfin tea party just lately blown to oblivion. Back on the beach, the cormorant opened up its wings like the cross and made straight for night time.

Chapter 9

Just as Gwyn had predicted, by morning, a letter of notice had been pasted on the door and was soon being stared out by protest posters from around the walls. The market people were strung around in angry, earnest knots. Iwan was organising a petition; there was a call to hold a rally outside the council offices. Smoking as usual – a finger worrying the length of an old brass rule for measuring material – Mo leaned on her elbow and watched what was going on. They had a year there, more or less. The chain stores needed a central location. The council bigwigs, likely as not, had a soft spot for organic veg and would keep that stand; Gwyn's keys and the baker's too, were popular. All the rest could start packing.

Mari looked delicate as she elbowed her way through the crowd. She opened her stall and precisely put in place each precious stone. Mending a watch, Gwyn glanced up at her but she kept her head down. Mari could feel Mo's eyes on her back before she brought their tea over and sat down behind the counter on the three-legged stool where she always enjoyed their first cuppa. Mo's sizeable shape swallowed the stool. She looked away from the goods on sale and stubbed out her cigarette on the side of her cup, flicking ash onto the floor. Mari was fiddling a diamond brooch onto a scrap of dark velvet.

"Like it?" Mari asked.

Mo's eyes darted away. "Too showy... Bling, my kids'd call it."

"But your ruby wedding's coming up, isn't it?" Mari prodded Mo's weak spot. "Look at this..." The ruby leaked red like a wound. "This stone's for passion..."

"Huh! After three children and a triple bypass there's not a lot of that left," Mo sniffed. But she looked a little more interested. "It's *quite* pretty." She started gently kicking the counter. "How come you don't sell anything..."

"What?"

"Well, something useful." She fumbled in the packet for another smoke but changed her mind. "Talk about useful, me and Dai, we've had a chat. He wants you to come in with us." The ruby ring warmed to Mari's rubbing. "We're together round the clock as it is anyway; might as well make it official. You can do the clothes and anything else you fancy; me and Dai'll stick to furniture. Between these walls, we could do OK." She paused. "There we are: said my piece."

A slant of light came through the hall's dirty windows. The ruby got hotter. Mo was expecting her answer. Mari realised selling jewellery was not what Mo counted as "useful". But to even think of giving it up! Mo's weight threatened to tip her off her stool. Mari shuffled up to her and held her arm. Their heads were close together.

"Thanks," Mari's voice dropped, "but I've got to say no."

Mo looked blankly past her. "We... we just want to make sure you're OK, that's all."

Mari swallowed. "I know. Thanks."

"You've got to face facts: it's going to happen."

Mari nodded and squeezed Mo's arm. Her friend was disappointed.

"I'll be OK... You know me."

Mo held her gaze. "OK," Mo said, getting up. Mari pulled her hand away. "Like a mule, you are. I knew that's what you'd say... Told Dai, I did... she's like a mule! And I'll tell you another thing. Don't think I could stand you full time anyway..." She went back over to her own stall.

"We can still do the evenings together!"

"Do what you want." Mo bent over her merchandise. "You always do: you can't teach an old dog..."

Mari smiled at her burrowing, bobtail high.

"Excuse me."

The man at Mari's counter, cap in hand, was crook-backed. She gave him a smile. She'd briefly seen him in the café first thing, getting browbeaten by Iwan. The cap was being wrung right out. He felt around in his suit pocket for a threadbare hankie tied at one end. His skin was sewn tight around his skull. When he put down the package, Mari glanced at him for permission to open it up. Laid out before her were a diamond engagement ring and two brooches. Mari's fingertips brushed the ring.

The man's nervous fingers were wearing out his trouser pocket. Thieves send out old people to sell stuff for them but greed invariably makes them ignore the taboo on a widower selling a wedding band. There was no wedding ring in this handkerchief: the old man was true to his vows. Crumbs were gathered at the corners of his mouth; his breath was sour. He didn't exactly stink, but was one of those people whose personal scent was broadcast louder than others. She'd seen him here before, hadn't she? Just not lost like this, like a widowed goose.

"Two hundred and fifty," Mari offered.

He put out his hand and Mari dipped into the money bag around her waist. Why was he so silent? She liked being a repository of people's love secrets: where they got engaged; the wedding; how many children, and how long their marriage had lasted. To tell the story helped in letting go: she was a good listener who had seen how an old man's eyes can be kindled by sharing his life story. This one, though, was far too quiet.

Mari counted out the ten-pound notes. Missing his trouser pocket a couple of times, the old man finally managed to push home his money. He put his cap back on and turned away vaguely, reluctant to leave the stand. As though weighed down by the wad of notes, he wandered over to the doors.

His bent shape slotted among the straight backs of the crowd. The seller had to leave before she could put away new stock. Gwyn noticed Mari watching the widower. Then she picked up the hanky and felt its weight; as the door slammed shut, a gust of wind sent the keys on Gwyn's stall rattling.

Chapter 10

The wind was sharp that morning; Mari was picking flowers from her front garden. The sea was a silver band; the sun a medallion. Snowdrops and daffodils had waxed and waned in a mild midwinter that had slid into a weirdly warm spring. Her back was bowed like a scythe as she sought out a smattering of bloom within the thick new leaf of the hedge. Catkins of pussy willow and hazel caught the light like earrings: grey-silver droplets and knuckles of pale gold that twisted on an updraught. The beech was flirting its little fans of beaten neon-green at her: she caught the twigs and bound them up in string.

Pollen was a fine gold dust all over her jumper. She made a posy of pale yellow primrose. Nanw was inside, copying her movements and squealing until Mari came up to the window to show her the contents of her cache. Then the monkey stood still to look properly, her hands a tight roll around her tail. Mari smiled, went back and forth to the cottage to fetch her purse and cardigan, locked the door and was out into her car without a backward glance.

The graveyard was beyond the village, overlooking the sea. Mari hated making the trip at Whitsun when you couldn't move for swooning families wielding plastic-wrapped Madonna lilies. Spin ahead a week and the bouquets were spent, just like the memories of those mourners who had sped on ahead into their lives. Mari plucked out her offerings and closed the passenger door.

She pushed open the black gate. The path doddered

41

between graves, tripping over them where they fell askew, exhausted as they were by the earth's insistence on pulling them under. They had cracked, and spindly claws of grass were forcing them open further. A rabbit scudded away. The church was a bright whitewash with slits to keep the wind out. The big doors put a ragged clump of desiccated daffodil into blue shade. Mari clutched her flowers closer.

There was a time when she'd come here every week but she hadn't been in a while, so every little change loomed large. She needn't ever visit again should she just take Mo's advice and leave him a shop-bought everlasting arrangement. Mo had been a proper anchor since they'd met: more like a sister, really. Both women seemed so different, but underneath, their pulses had the same counts per minute. Gusts of air tugged at her clothes and tumbled the birds over into acrobatics. They had bruised her primrose petals a little. At the far end of the cemetery were newer graves, only a field above the clifftop.

The tombstone in the corner was bare save a few dry stalks from Mari's last tribute. She threw them out and went to fetch fresh water from the tap by the hedge, in the older section which was nearly full. As a girl, when her father was in a good mood, they would walk together through the village and down to the beach. On their way back, if it was hot and she was thirsty, they would call in here for water. He'd read out the inscriptions and they'd both try and recall them as they went home.

Her jug was overflowing. She went back and filled the pot for her bouquet of beech. The jar was shallow and heavy, designed to resist the worst of raging winter storms set on upending the whole churchyard into the sea, floral memorials and all. Mari crouched down and sat on the kerb of the grave. Serene, with eyes closed, she turned her face up to the breeze. Sometimes she'd talk to him, like she would at prayer. She'd tell him what had been going on, or she would hear his voice. She had been disappointed, too, having sat so long like some stone angel just to wrench herself home weeping then wake from the terror of his face rotting in earth. The memory made her seasick. But at times her vigil might reveal him in a vision of his son, Dafydd. Himself, caught within a smile or gesture of his own flesh and blood. Today, though, the grave was still.

"What's wrong with you?" The wind gave another deep breath out. Her eyes were open. Was he sulking because she'd kept away so long? She shut her eyes again and tried to focus on his voice, his hair, his face. The strength of this gale was against her. She succeeded in remembering the times he'd helped her and Mo clear houses, or had driven out with her to auctions that would otherwise have been too far away. Other scenes evaded her. She opened her eyes once more, exasperated. He was as quiet today as that hump-backed little man with his bundle of keepsakes he wouldn't be keeping. Mari stared irritably at the sea.

A blackthorn in the hedge was hunched against the wind – and yet it was still growing. It stooped over towards the church, roots holding on despite being blown the wrong way. It resembled a wizened bride, white confetti against her charred bones. Mari listened to the wind. No sign. Usually by now both their voices would be humming. Her shoulders drooped and a chill passed through her. She got up, brushing her skirt.

"I'll be back when you're feeling better."

She picked up her primroses and took the jug back to the tap. The grave was shining black and solemn despite the gaiety of its green tiara. Mari frowned. Walking along the rows of tombstones, she glanced at any new ones. The names on some of them were those of households she and Mo had cleared. *Gwyn*! She stepped back and stood still. "Ann, dear wife of Gwyn..." Mari peered at the grave. That must be Gwyn from the market's wife! She felt dizzy. The stone was new; the grave newly cut and shin-deep in flowers. She thought of what he'd said at the shoreline.

She stepped over a low stone wall leading to a rough patch outside the church bounds. A few tiny stone markers and little crosses: no names, no flowers. No sign of life at all, whether mourner, visitor, or merely a mower come to trim the lawn. She placed the primroses in a nest of long grass, their open yellow beaks upturned in hope.

Chapter 11

Whack! The hammer came down. The old hall was packed with people hoping for rich pickings. Mari would have preferred not to have missed a day at the market, but there were only one or two of these police auctions a year. After all, she might find something here for Dafydd's birthday. She hadn't seen him for a while, and thinking of a present made her feel closer to him. Mari scanned the sale listings. So many valuable items had been stolen: if the police found them but couldn't trace the owner in time, they could be sold. Today the choice of jewellery was excellent; clocks, too and one or two neat little dressers.

It was usually drugs that drove young men to theft: they didn't have a clue about the stuff they had to offload. Now and then you came across a thief with especially good taste. Mari combed through the catalogue as things got under way. Nothing major here... If these items were all part of the same stash, this robber was quite the connoisseur of art deco jewellery: surely he stole to order? Whoever he was, he was in love with jewels, just the same as she was.

The next lot came under the hammer. The auctioneer was babbling in his own language, his eyes a magpie swooping for meaning among the faces in front of him. He collected and converted gestures into currency: a wink; a tipped cap; a nudged elbow, even merely the cast of an eye. Figures filled the air rather than words: your name didn't matter – nor where you came from – in this exciting exchange of vows.

"Are you buying?" An elderly lady spoke breathlessly. "I'm

late and I haven't got the number. I want..." She took a catalogue out of her handbag, her hands shaking as she flipped the pages. "Can you help me?"

Her lot was next.

Mari agreed. "How high can you go?"

"Three hundred."

It was a silver crucifix from the twenties, studded with quite sizeable diamonds. Crosses hadn't been popular then: must be pretty rare. It wouldn't be easy to get it at that price, not with the kind of London vultures you got here – all smart suits and flashy phones – used to handling thousands' worth of jewellery a week. The price went up in ten-pound gradations: Mari kept absolutely still. She hardly noticed when the woman clutched her arm to peer over people's heads in the row ahead. Mari raised a hand at two hundred and fifty, but a dealer tapped his nose at three hundred and ten. The lady nudged her: Mari raised her price again. People were talking about the next lot.

"Did you get it?" The woman seemed confused.

"Yes."

"It's perfect."

"It's a lovely piece."

"Do you know much about crucifixes?"

Mari smiled. "My father was a vicar."

"Well, no wonder you've turned out a proper lady. I'll go and pay now so we're square." Mari looked in the catalogue for the next lot while she waited for the woman to come back. She saw a familiar figure. The adrenaline started pumping as she made her decision to approach him.

"Gwyn."

His face was lit by a warm smile.

"Mari..." One hand was tucked around a package; in his other, a printed number on card.

"There's some nice stuff here." Mari's voice was small and tight.

"A clock," he said. "Don't know if I need more stock, but it's a hobby..."

Mari agreed and glanced at his wedding ring.

He looked calmly at her. "Mari..."

"Yes?"

The little old lady had come back. "There we are... Look! Isn't it lovely?" She showed them the cross shining coldly in its box.

Gwyn smiled politely. "Excuse me. My lot's next."

"Oh, sorry," the woman started.

"Not at all," he moved away.

Mari looked at the space left behind him as the woman chattered on. "Here you are: something to bring you luck!" She pressed a hot two-pound coin into Mari's hand.

"You don't need –"

"No: take it. I wouldn't have got it if it hadn't been for you."

"Well, I hope it makes you very happy."

"Oh, no. It's not for me." She put the box and her purse into her bag. "My granddaughter's getting baptised on Sunday. Wanted her to have something to remind her of it – and of me! We don't live forever, do we?"

Mari kept an eye on Gwyn over on the other side of the room.

"Mark a new life... a clean slate... Nice, isn't it? Thanks again." She touched Mari's arm lightly and turned to go.

Mari's smile stayed fixed as she watched the old woman making her way past a policemen at the exit. She thought of that innocent soul starting out on life's journey with a stolen cross at her throat.

Chapter 12

As soon as she got home from work, Mari started laundering and repairing the vintage costumes ready for sale. Out the wet clothes went on a line across the back garden. Her hands were red from rubbing the heavy material in the warm water. She'd let Nanw out of her cage and put her collar on so that she could sit on the table close by.

She had all sorts of different clothes: gorgeous gloves far too small for women today: skirts; petticoats; underwear, indeed whole outfits from head to toe – from fancy combs to silk stockings. How little Dafydd used to love dressing up in hat and waistcoat... She'd have to be extra careful with these silk items and fringed shawls.

They were all so tiny – she certainly couldn't fit into them – and yet there was such a demand among collectors, especially those connected to the theatre or museums, or that rare woman with a waist small enough to actually wear them. Those were her favourite buyers: slim women smitten by a piece, profit the last thing on their mind. The nightie she was washing had aged a dirty yellow. Next she had to mend a dress saved from moths who'd been treating it as a midnight snack. All it needed on close inspection was to renew the collar with a bit of ribbon.

Among her stock she also had dressy bags: velvet encrusted with pearls or embroidered with beads. Those should sell. She had spent the previous night making space in the passageway. Her favourites – outfits for special occasions and a couple of bridal gowns – still lined the wall but now had more breathing room. The clothes outside were alive on the line as though their new owners were dancing in them right now. She smiled. Nanw was getting restless. Mari wrung out the water from the nightdress, draping it over her arm to peg it out into the only gap left. The sun was too weak to dry them properly but at least they'd get an airing.

She wiped her hands on her apron and watched the clothes drip. Mari caught Nanw's arm, took down a bagful of nuts together with three egg cups and lined up the latter. Straightaway Nanw started chattering. Mari took a nut and put it under a cup, making sure the monkey hadn't seen which. Nanw always sat still then, pure concentration. Mari moved them around and slid them back in a different order.

"Come on then, Nanw love: where's the nut?"

The monkey's eyebrows went up and down as she looked down the row. Often she would knock them all over, one by one, before she found it. Whenever she succeeded, she yelped and jumped on the spot, holding her tail.

The pair played together until dusk fell and Mari was worn out laughing. She was sure Nanw was getting the hang of it. The monkey had lost her temper during their last game, throwing the egg cups up in the air and making a grab for the food. Mari got to her before she had a chance to mess up the whole kitchen, and back to her cage went the tricksy bundle. Mari sat by the best-room window with her sewing box and the frock. Her tongue poked out on one side as she attempted to thread the needle. Her eyesight must be getting weaker. She sucked one thread end to a point and managed it this time, tying the other in a knot. She'd have to replace both ribbons. She started ripping out the stitches from underneath with a sharp hook.

Someone had made these neat stitches once. Where, and for what grand party? A puff of dust rose as each little loop snapped. Whenever she stopped to rest her eyes, her mind kept creeping over to the emerald squirrelled deep in the box beside her and she had to drag it back to her mending. The cat stuck her head in then went out again to sit by Nanw's cage in the bedroom. Just as she did every other night, she sat whipping her tail in and out of the bars, just beyond the monkey's reach.

Mari had created two tidy rows of tiny stitches along both ribbons, entirely concealing the moths' sabotage. She rubbed her nape and shook out the dress to get a proper look. It was a picture: pink silk with tiny buttons all down the back. The waist was a handspan; the detail on the collar and the new ribbons suited it perfectly. She slotted her needle into the lid of the sewing box and folded up the frock.

In the corridor she took out a cardboard box full of clothes. She'd have to sell these off cheaply. She flapped the covers closed: out of sight, out of mind. The place was starting to empty; it felt odd to have so much room. She breathed in deeply and remembered the clothes on the line. She checked on her pets: the cat was sleeping soundly while Nanw was trying to snatch at that tantalising tail. Mari went over and tapped Nanw's hand. The monkey drew back her arm and nursed it as though it were gravely injured. Mari let out a sigh of long-suffering, and stared into the dark outside.

A rustle at the window. Mari's breath was trapped in her breast. Smeared into a Halloween mask against the glass was a face, hollows for eyes, its mouth a gaping "O". Someone was in the front garden! Sara had become as thin and pale as a stick of chalk, and she was looking in at Mari and the monkey. Mari took a step back, turned on her heels and rushed to the back of the house. Nanw had started screeching, making the cat snarl and show her teeth. Mari folded her legs up on the floor and clasped them tightly as though she were a small box anyone coming over the back wall would miss. Staying at the back of the house to make sure the figure had definitely gone, she started to wonder whether it hadn't all been a dream brought on by too much close work. She was cold by the time she unpacked herself. Nanw was quiet. Mari forced herself to look out the back. Staring into the darkness, she saw nothing except a row of lively moonlit shapes, beckoning.

Chapter 13

Mari hadn't told anyone about the face at the window, especially not Mo, who would only think she was going mad. Anyway, shock had smelted the memory so that it was just a molten mess in her mind. By seven a.m. Mari was on her way to auction with Mo and Dai to sell the things they'd had from that church. There'd been a public viewing at the hall the previous week. Mari wasn't that bothered about the auction itself, but she was in need of company.

"They're letting Ann stay on at the market," Mo mumbled between mouthfuls of Marmite sandwich wrapped in greaseproof paper. She passed one to Dai.

"Ann Chips?"

"Yes. But they're making her move into a new unit."

"Oh."

"The same with Alan Veg."

"Yeah, him," Dai said as he changed gear with one hand and fed himself bread with the other. "He's related to that councillor."

"And don't forget Gwyn..."

"What?"

"Gwyn... they say he's providing a service or something..." Mo pushed her glasses back up her nose and ate her last piece of bread.

"He didn't tell me anything."

"That's what he's like. I haven't got a peep out of him in years. Up to him if he wants to be like that..."

"Might not be his fault..."

"A smile doesn't cost anything," Mo interrupted. "You're too soft for your own good." She brushed off the breadcrumbs. "But there you go: he's landed on his feet again."

Mo lit up a cigarette each for herself and Dai to cap the perfect breakfast.

Two heavy grates propped the back doors open. Pencils at the ready, people circled the entrance like carrion crows. Dai gave some mates a thumbs-up and backed up the van as close as possible.

Mo and Mari slithered out and went to wander around while Dai had the help of the men to unload. They had brought what would be one of the centrepieces: church pews, polished and piled in a stack to be sold in separate lots.

Beds; cupboards; tablecloths; two linen presses, and pine washstands that would come up lovely after a bath in caustic soda, crowned with a floral bowl and jug. Mari ran her finger along some beading on a wardrobe. Wouldn't a new piece be nice for the cottage? Her ceilings were too low though, and her doorways too narrow.

Over in the corner, Mo was chatting to one of the local lads whose job it was to clear out the furniture afterwards. The room had filled up quickly. There were a few young couples looking for a bargain to start setting up home. The woman would choose and the man would do the bidding in a hesitant sort of way while she hung onto his arm trying to see what was going on. The antique dealers were also here, muffled up warm, an eye out for an unlikely-looking item to be buffed up and sold in town with a hefty mark-up. They had been panning the countryside for its gold so long there was only the odd nugget left to be had, for a price, at this sort of sale. Mo was following the buyers around. She stopped when she saw a settle with a lid on its deep seat.

"Fancy it?" Mari asked.

"Mam had one out in the garden." Mo's face had softened. "Dat had made holes along it so the hens could lay in them. It was my job to fetch the eggs, and they would still be warm." Mo raised the seat and peered in. "They were tasty, too. Could only afford meat on Sundays and Mam used to add flour to make our mash go further, but at breakfast we dined like kings!" She looked so happy, Mari smiled. Mo let the lid close. "What a way to treat antiques! None of us realised their value then, see. We got rid of grandfather clocks too – worth a fortune, can you believe it?"

"Hundred. One hundred. Do I have fifty? One hundred and fifty pounds." Rap! Excitement was escalating. Dai stood at the front, writing down what prices their stuff had sold at. The women returned to the rear to explore the jumble. There was not much there that would sell on. Mari went behind a huge plywood cupboard and stopped dead.

She had found a sort of vanitas, under glass. The case held a slice of nature in 3D: a rabbit grazing by a tree stump, gazing through blue glass eyes forever at a field of flowers. That fur would be so smooth and alive... Up on the stump, though, was a fox: forepaws placed to spring, teeth whetted for the soft flesh waiting below. Those pretty flowers had cast their charm: the rabbit was oblivious. The fox had its prey fixed in its sights and had all the time in the world to enjoy the kill.

"What is it?"

"Oh! Nothing..."

Mo looked past her. "Mm, charming! Come on, Dai wants a second breakfast. Our stuff's all sold."

"Oh, OK then."

"Are you all right?" Mo asked.

"Of course..."

"You look like you could do with a rest. Come on, I'll get you some nice sugary tea."

Mo led her out by the arm through the crowd. Dai had rolled up his money and was snapping an elastic band around it; Mo said her goodbyes. Mari felt the relief of fresh air. Off they drove, Dai promising to treat them. Mari couldn't forget that innocent little rabbit, spellbound by beauty, the nape of its neck laid open to harm.

Chapter 14

Those jewels were giving Mari a hard time. They were supposed to be healing, but having to set them out on her stall after a sleepless night was making her brain fit to burst. She had brought in all the clothes that were destined for the sale rail. They had been given priority over the jewellery, right at the front of the stand: the white gloves hand in hand; the pink frock glad again to act the party girl and welcome all comers. Mari piled up the bags on one side of the glass counter and wrote out the price on a card.

Nanw, apparently in constant pain, had kept her on her toes. Mari decided to keep a low profile until she started feeling better. Mo was busy with bargain-hunters snapping up multiples of items you couldn't get in the big shops. In Mari's hand was the sheet of stickers Iwan had given her first thing: Save Our Market.

"Mari?" She looked up. Gwyn was right in front of her.

"I... I th... thought maybe," he said, going red, "you could," Mari's heart came beating loud, "Maybe you could..." Mo looked over at them both, surprised to see him talking to someone. "I'm looking for a few gemstones."

"Oh! Of course."

"I need twelve," Gwyn said. Mari searched around for a pencil. "It's n... not a big order. Twelve little gemstones... for a dolls' house. To make a clock out of a watch. Nothing too expensive: it's for the numbers. I'll set them..."

"Fine. All the same colour or...?"

"No, different... be prettier." Mari nodded. "Well then!" he finished and turned to go.

"I... I heard you can stay on," Mari said, thinking maybe guilt had stopped him mentioning it.

"Yes."

"Great! You must be pleased." He looked uncertain. Despite herself, she said, "Your wife must be really pleased, mustn't she?"

He nodded awkwardly and went away. Mari's headache was bringing out the big guns now. Her forehead felt bunched up under her skull, like flannel in a seamstress' fingers.

Mo brought over a cuppa and set it in front of her. "Here you are," she said. "You've got to slow down, Mari, love. You look green around the gills!"

Mo went back over to her stall where some old boy was hovering and she fluttered her fingers at him like a flirt.

The sound of someone shouting made Mari shiver. Mo turned back to find out where the noise was coming from. Mari felt her breastbone tighten and her legs felt as though they were about to give under her.

"What've you been telling my lad?" The pitch of Sara's voice was dangerous. Dafydd's mother was a thin strip of nothing, raw-boned and pale as dust. Her dark eyes were ringed about with shadow. Customers and shopkeepers alike were eavesdropping. "Mari! What've you been telling my lad?"

Gwyn looked over at Mari, puzzled.

"Go home now," Mari said to Sara quietly, her cheeks colouring up.

"What?"

"Don't make such a big fuss..."

"Don't you tell me what to do! My husband might have liked a bossy woman but it's not going to wash with me, right?"

Mari's blood was churning like surf.

"Come on, now… Go home. We can talk properly another time…"

"Talk?" Sara spat. "I've had it up to here with your talk! You've already filled Dafydd's head with nonsense." Gwyn was hovering not too far away. "Well, who's this, then: another boyfriend?" Sara turned back to Mari and continued, "I came over to see you." Mari looked down at the floor. "He wants to give up the butcher's… go away… leave that girlfriend of his. You're going to take my son away from me too, aren't you?" Sara was lost, like a loose thread on a plush coat. She pulled her dirty jumper down at the back. "He needs to look after the business…" Her face was haggard.

Mari couldn't help picking at an old scab. "Look after?" she asked with a half-smile. She noticed the caretaker at their side.

"Don't you laugh at me. This is all your fault, I'm telling you!" The caretaker stepped in front of Sara. Shoppers were whispering in groups or dragging their young children away. "Why can't you just leave us alone? Why d'you pick on us?" she shouted over the caretaker's shoulder. He grabbed her and she started screeching and kicking even more. Dafydd arrived with a black eye, out of breath. He took hold of his mother and managed to calm her down.

"Don't, Mam… please… don't… hush." He was flushed; his shoulders weighed down by all this unwelcome attention. The whites of his eyes seemed very bright as he flashed a glance at Mari. Dafydd led his mother away.

"Show's over," Mo shouted at the crowd.

"It was her that killed him!" Sara shouted. Mo was trying to comfort Mari but they had both heard her parting shot. Gwyn wavered then turned his back. People were drifting away. Mo tried to hold Mari's hand. "It was her that killed him!" Sara's words were like smoke on the air.

"Mari. Don't... don't listen to her," Mo said. "You know what she is."

Mari looked her in the eye. "Perhaps she's right..."

"Mari... don't," Mo started. Mari turned to put the jewellery away.

"Shut the stall up for me?" she asked, shoving past Mo and rushing out, box in arms. Mo turned to her friend's counter and collected the cup of tea which was cold, with a slight skin on it.

Chapter 15

She tipped the Bible onto the floor and took the lid off the box. Out came the soft toys, spilling all over the place. She heard Nanw complaining – she didn't like change and was annoyed with Mari for having come home early.

Mari felt heavy and listless. The look in Dafydd's eyes was engraved onto her mind. That was the horror of love: your sweetheart could stick a knife into your eyeball and sharpen it a notch every chance they got. The only thing to save you then was trust that they wouldn't use that power against you.

Mari's breathing was sharp and shallow. She snatched the bundle with its hard little core from the depths of the chest. She took the jewel out from shadow and felt its outline through the swaddling. She stood up with creaking bones and took it over to the desk where she set it in a pool of lamplight. Her hands shook as she opened up the package: a chip of grave-cloth green.

She cleared a workspace, fetched wax. She began her sacrament by washing the stone in alcohol. She worked quickly, tension tightening soft flesh to muscle and sinew. Her throat had shut fast, stopping her from answering Nanw's animal cries. She sat down at the old cutting wheel and whipped away the shroud of a sheet that kept it clear of cold and dust. The wheel was smooth, it was an old friend; Mari adjusted the settings so she could start her ministrations. She was all instinct. She lit a candle and dripped wax to fix the stone to the metal spoke. Her tools seemed sterile: she was a surgeon about to take a scalpel to the tiny cold heart. The flame began to heat the gemstone, and Mari too felt warmed by that old smell of wax. The wheel was baptised in a sprinkling of water. She started up the machine, that turning sound signalling something was about to change shape.

The sweat was warm on her back. She tried to still her hands. Closing her eyes to the candlelight, hers was a prayer muttered against the rumble of the revolving wheel. The humming took her up to somewhere far from this room with its unwelcome guest at the window. She sought His help to scour from her brain each inch of that lean white face. Down on the scratching wheel went the emerald's cheek.

It let out only a rustle of leaves shimmying in the breeze. Diamonds always whined and howled and clawed like creatures possessed, but the emerald yielded only a whisper. Mari felt the itch of those scabs she had inside her as she methodically set to skinning the gemstone. She was sculptress; she was mistress now, and the woes of the world simply faded out. An eye glowed at her from one side of the dark coal: a green wound aweep with molten lava. The balm of this lustre was bestowed on Mari's own eyes and she had never felt so calm. Light penetrating a jewel is of the purest kind: Mari felt blessed by its clean reflection. It lit up gold the dust she brushed from the jewel.

Any stone has an immanent spirit which can only be seen once a facet is cut. Then you can see the imperfections. The candle guttered in the whoosh of the wheel which worked on widening the gemstone's window, polishing the surface and also clearing the hurt from Mari's head and heart. She had never felt so unburdened. She was almost drunk on the rustling sound and the flow of light. The window was crystal clear now, no hiding place for any flaws. When the whirring stopped, she blew on the wax to soften it and peeled the gem from its tallow nest, wiping it with an old rag. She turned the machine off at the switch. Silence. Mari's body was weightless, the jewel luminous on her palm as she fetched a glass to magnify its interior. It was only now that she realised how upset Nanw sounded. She was screaming and rattling the bars of her cage. Mari ignored her anyway, raised the glass and brought the gemstone up to the light. Mari looked right into the emerald and stared into its own green eye.

She stiffened, her head fizzing. The stone had a birthmark! In the midst of velvety green was a fingerprint – a bubble of air in a perfect pattern. She tracked the twisting tracery trapped in there. She gripped the table to stop herself giving way. Mari blinked away. A blooming foliage they called "garden" is quite common in an emerald but a single fingerprint is rare. The inclusion would make the gem easy to break but so lovely if she managed to cut it right.

The crash of furniture being knocked over broke her free from thoughts of the stone. It sounded as though the bedroom was being wrecked. She ran over, slipping the jewel into her apron pocket. Nanw had escaped from the cage and had ruined her own bedding. Ornaments had been smashed, blankets shredded and the floor used as a toilet. The monkey was crouched among broken pottery, panting. The ebony box had been tipped out from under the bed. Her own childhood photos all over the place. Mari felt cold as stone. The monkey screeched and bared her teeth, then moaned and reached out her arms towards her mistress. Mari peered – uncertainly – into the little black eyes and then she bent and picked Nanw up.

Chapter 16

She'd had only the briefest snatches of scratchy sleep. These had taken Mari into a child's-eye solar system where air bubbles made an orbit round her sun like a handspan of green ink fingerprints. She'd woken in a soak of sweat and went to the best room to check on the real emerald. When she cut it, she would treat its weak spot as a mark of true-born beauty. Lack of maternal attention was Nanw's excuse for whingeing and rattling the bars. The cat gave the monkey a wide berth, looping herself around Mari's legs like an insecure scarf.

Mari hadn't been back to the market since the incident. Fatigue was making her vague: she couldn't settle down to pray despite the best part of a morning spent on her knees, trying to rid her mind of every last shard of that emerald. She had neither eaten nor drunk properly for days.

Mari's father had taught her to pray: almost every day she had sought forgiveness and given thanks. He made her kneel on the flagged kitchen floor longer than was kind, to instil in her gratitude. How her poor knees had suffered until she'd hit on the idea of stuffing hankies down her socks. But one fell out and Father had caned her on the legs. She'd had some lecture about how great the suffering of Jesus had been, how little, in comparison, that of her knees. Why then had she to suffer at all, she'd asked, if it was Jesus' job to do it for all our sakes?

She'd had to endure weeks embroidering a ceremonial cope under the tutelage of Miss Jones next door. Maybe Father thought this was a proper chastisement for a girl. Even though she was already enduring one finger-numbing punishment,

Mari had had a second – a clip on the ear from Miss Jones – when she chose the question, "Why's Daddy's cloak so fancy when Jesus just wore rags?" She hadn't repeated that particular gem.

Oddly though, Mari grew to like sewing. She'd sink into meditation, letting her mind wander across continents and subjects. A young girl at prayer could get away with all sorts of thoughts, which was handy since Father still wasn't averse to using his cane.

Mari tried once more to concentrate. She prayed for help in facing the changes at the market, and for Mo and Dai. For Sara, and for Dafydd on the brink of manhood. The soul of the young woman and of those in all the other photos. She prayed for Nanw, and for Gwyn. For those remembered on their brand-new crosses and those almost forgotten on the skew-whiff gravestones scuffed to no name by sea winds. It went on and on until all warmth went out of her, sending Mari into a limbo with only the clock's tick for company.

Mo tapped on the door. She had been calling by every day while Mari was away but hadn't yet got a response. Peering through the heavy drapes, Mo's calls made Nanw jitter and Mari open her eyes onto darkness.

Mari tried to get up but her legs wouldn't support her. She lurched forwards into the fireplace, knocking a mirror off it so that it smashed onto the tiled floor.

"Mari! Mari! Open the door, girl. Mari!" Mari pulled herself up, registering the urgency. The pad of her thumb was cut. "Mari!" What should she do? Nanw's cage stank and needed cleaning. Rubbing her head and trying to stop herself shivering, she hobbled over to the door. "Mari! Come here." Mo pushed past her. She gripped her friend by the shoulders. "What's going on?"

"I w... was just..."

"Shshsh now... you'll be OK, come on, come on. Look at your hand." Mo guided her onto the bed, leaving her to come round while she got dinner started. Back she came, rubbing her hands against Mari's to warm them. "Shshsh," Mo murmured. She saw the mirror in pieces. "Well now you've gone and got yourself seven years' bad luck. At least you're not superstitious like me. Well! Let's get you a nice wash and brush up while the spuds are on. You're as white as that pillow." Mari waited for Mo to fetch hot water then pulled off her nightie over her head, making Nanw laugh. Mo found fresh underwear in a drawer, together with a warm jumper and trousers. She saw how awkwardly Mari was bending. Mo gently pushed her back down and pulled on a pair of clean socks for her. "Well, aren't you posh now?" She washed Mari's cut in salt water, smoothing a plaster down over it. She went to mash the potatoes with a bit of butter and salt, returning with platefuls for them both. "Listen. Eat up and stop this nonsense." Mari wouldn't let her in the house whenever she succumbed to the blues, and so Mo hadn't been near the place for months. Whenever they arranged to go for a walk together, Mari would wait for her outside. Mo noticed the photos on the mantelpiece: a whole shelf of strangers. "Don't get into a fret over what happened at the market," Mo went on. "Water under the bridge." Mari hadn't taken a mouthful yet. "All ancient history, anyway! That woman needs to move on." Sitting down beside Mari, Mo loaded her fork with fluffy goodness.

Mari flushed and put down her knife. "But what if she's right and it *was* my fault he died?" she asked quietly.

"Well she isn't!"

"But..."

"It was an accident... that's all."

"But he was coming over to see me," Mari persisted. "If we'd not..."

"You just can't think like that! 'If only we'd done this, what if we'd done the other...' Pointless! We get the one path in life and that's it. Your paths crossed, didn't they?" Mari relaxed and Mo went on, her face softening when she saw how open her expression was. "His time had come: no one could have done anything..."

Silence.

"I know she's been stopping him coming to see me," Mari said.

"Dafydd?"

Mari nodded. "Well, he'll be twenty-one before long: old enough to look after his own business."

Mo tucked into the meal, leaning, without realising why, away from Nanw.

"She was so skinny," Mari said.

"Why didn't you tell me she'd been here?"

"I... I don't know. People talk..."

"People say all sorts of rubbish... Tuck in, now. You need to build up your strength – forget all that claptrap." Mo made everything seem simple. "You can never move on if you're stuck in the past." Mari nodded. "Eat up, come on. We'll light a big fire, get this place snug and tidy."

By mid-afternoon, Mari looked a bit better. Mo had handwashed some clothes and hung them on the line. Nanw's cage had been cleaned and the bedclothes changed. Mari felt stronger so she hid away the emerald at the bottom of the box. Mo was singing as she wiped the kitchen table.

After Mo had reluctantly left her alone, Mari mixed some milk with a drop of brandy from a dusty bottle stashed in the kitchen. She set it to warm above the fireplace and opened the cage to let the monkey sit in her lap while she had her drink. Nanw's arms were a hoop around Mari's neck, her head tucked in under her chin. It was nearly dark. Mari lay back

68

on the bed with a happy Nanw, nosetip touching nose, one gaze wrapped in the other's as though it were a gift shared. Leathery hands combing human hair, both close to sleep. But before she closed her eyes, Mari saw a terrible sadness in the monkey's uncomprehending eyes.

Chapter 17

Mari went back to work a couple of days later. Of course the fuss had been forgotten, just as Mo had predicted. Because of its size, few shoppers at the market had witnessed what had happened, and her efforts to hold her head up high went unnoticed. It had got much quieter though, the talk of closing down acting as deterrent. Still, they enjoyed themselves. Mari and Mo ordered cake at teatime and chewed the fat over the fate of the market. Iwan joined them. Committees were going through the motions of debating the matter, he said, but no one really held out much hope. Dafydd's stall had been shuttered up and no one had seen hide nor hair of him for days. Must be busy looking after his mother, Mari told herself.

When the day was done, the women got into Mo's car, leaving town for the next valley.

"Dafydd's birthday next week," Mari said, holding her box as usual.

Mo was trying to interpret the directions scrawled on a scrap torn from a packet of detergent. The landscape stretched out flat in both directions.

"Is it?" She stuffed the cardboard back into the side of the door. "I have my twenty-first every year."

Mo wound down the window and stuck her hand out into the air rushing past. Mari let herself relax.

"Got a couple of things for the picnic already," Mari went on. "I bet it stays fine – he's always lucky."

Mo kept quiet. She and Dai had just decided to leave the market by the end of summer. But since she hadn't seen Mari so upbeat in months, it seemed bad timing to break the news right then.

The farm would have been remote when it had been built, but each year a row of houses marched closer. The road there was half lane, with a strip of green lawn down its back. Mo parked the car in the yard and fished for the right key.

"We haven't done a farmhouse for ages," Mo said. The garden path was crooked but the shrubs were well-manicured. Vegetables were shoulder to shoulder, like soldiers, on an oblong plot plentifully fortified with compost. A metal bucket had been recruited as a plantpot and set flowering on the wall of the pigsty. The door had been neatly painted dark blue. Mo shouldered it open and the pair stood in silent prayer. Then Mo's heels tapped along the tan-and-black chequerboard of the empty entrance hall. Mari scored a finger along the floral wallpaper and raised the latch of the low door into the dining room. This was a small room with one deep-set window overlooking the yard. The few jugs were not on the dresser but dangled by hooks on the salting rods in the ceiling. The floor was clean-swept flagging; apart from horse brasses either side of the fireplace, there was no other ornament or furniture here. Strung up above the mantelpiece was a pockmarked mirror. If you swung it to one side, it left an oval "O" against a wall yellowed by years of hearth smoke.

They would have passed meals hand-to-hand from kitchen to dining room, through the hatch. The kitchen was all fifties cupboards in light blue, their upper doors engraved with egg shapes in frosted glass. Cutlery had been bundled up in knives and forks already. Mo shot a frown at her. Up the narrow stairs were two little bedrooms you had to go through to reach the bathroom, and off that a third. The lack of decoration upstairs dampened Mari's mood. Mo was on the landing, marking her cross on the linen press.

"Not much to do here, is there?" asked Mo.

Mari ducked under a low beam supporting the spine of the sloping ceiling. Everything had been packed for storage, all carpets rolled away and beds made up. In the furthest bedroom, the blankets on the single bed had been stretched into hospital corners so tight they would injure any invalid. A bedside table: a glimpse of a Bible, a book on gardening and reading glasses, before she shut the drawer on it. There was a large desk set in the narrow window. Mari's fingers worried the ink that was blooming in the woodgrain. These, and the inkspots marring the floor, were the only stains in the house.

Mari opened one of the desk drawers. Envelopes which had spent too long, too close in each other's company, breathed out in relief, evading her grasp and collapsing across the floor. Her cheeks flushed when she stooped to retrieve them. Here were names that were either notorious or ordinary: Siân Evans, Mr Jones, Lloyd George, Saunders Lewis. Her brow furrowed. There were hundreds: swimming pools'-worth of ink. The drawer was still stuffed. Mo was singing happily downstairs. Mari shut the door and hooked a finger into an envelope's armpit. A love letter to his first sweetheart in the village. Page on page of feeling. Warming to her curiosity, she opened another: a list of all the cars he'd owned. Mari's collar felt tight. Those familiar waves were whipping up in her stomach. The room was stifling. She jumped up to open the window then returned to her reading, her eyes skimming from line to line.

"Mari?"

She slammed the drawer closed, letting one letter slip into her skirt folds. Surely Mo would notice Mari's heart beating? The weakness had seized Mari again.

"You're quiet, aren't you?" Mo came in. "Look what I

found." She showed her a red ceramic picture frame decorated with the number fifty. "Seen him before?"

Mari picked up the picture frame. The couple were smiling happily, hands entwined, a knife hovering above the cake. She went pale. "The quiet man," she said, her voice guttering.

"What?" Mo asked, taking back the picture.

"I b... bought a few things off him a few months back – a ring and two brooches."

"Thought he looked familiar! All those people we see, though: they all look the same to me." Mo decided the wardrobe wasn't worth dragging to auction.

"What's that?" Mo pointed at the letter in her lap, ignoring the pile on the floor.

"Nothing..."

"Starting that collecting lark again, are you?" Mo asked, her eyes steady on Mari's face.

Mari could feel the paper fine as muslin in her palms. "No... but I'd better keep these."

Under Mo's gaze, Mari kept her eyes on the letter.

"Well if you've really got to..."

Mo turned away and went to finish her work in the other rooms while Mari scuttled to secrete her papers in a black bin bag and join Mo at the head of the stairs.

"That didn't take long, Mari... Ugh, it makes me feel sick."

"What does?"

"Getting everything ready like that."

"What d'you mean?"

"He hadn't any family left, had he? Cleared the place out himself."

"But how did he...?" Mari had reached the bottom step.

They both looked up the stairwell at the postage stamp of sky.

"Hanging. He packed it all up and then he hung himself."

Mo rubbed her arms and nudged her friend out of her way so that she could lock the door. A pair of swallows under the eaves were falling out over where to build their nest.

Chapter 18

The distant sky was a silver streak of mackerel that mid-morning. Up above it was bright blue, and against it the gorse was a hot yellow. There was more than a hint of summer in these seaside colours and in the almond scent. Mari's sleep had been broken, though, and she had awoken to the sound of Nanw moaning.

Right through the night following their day at the farmhouse, Mari had prayed for the quiet man. She had once held a hard and fast rule that you don't read other people's post. Accordingly, she had at first refused to let herself open even one more of those orderly letters. Then she'd sat on the bed among them for hours, just letting her movements shift those handwritten sheets so that his words began to whisper louder than the humble man himself had managed in the market. It was a whisper like that of her cutting wheel. After a couple of weeks, her steely sense of duty had softened and she found she could assess the angle of a K, skim for signs in a syntax and find the fissure in a clause like the craftswoman she was. She had been eking out the gaps between the letters, making herself a snack after coming in from work and only then sitting in silence with a stream of thoughts melting as salve along her fingers, a waxy trace of meaning having trailed across the bed.

The words were now mere powder on the wayside, leaving the man's soul scoured and shining. It lay naked on Mari's bed in a white pile of pages and empty envelopes. No wonder the widower had had no speech left when he'd come to sell his goods. Mari picked up once again the letter he had written to his wife when they'd realised they couldn't have children. She had been reading it over ever since first light. She was certain that, face to face with his wife, not one of those words would have surfaced. Mari was looking for the last letter to his dead wife, for an explanation of what finally pulled him under, but the letters were all mixed up now, nuggets from his youth and of his age all tumbling together. Mari rubbed her head and got up to make tea. When she went past the door, she thought maybe she'd heard someone outside, but it was just a light breeze flicking the leaves in the trees.

Dafydd's present, all wrapped up, was waiting on the kitchen table. Propped against it was a card in a clean white envelope. Mari had been worrying for weeks what to get him; in the end she had plumped for a simple chain of warm gold. It was antique, heavy, strong; its red colour would warm up the pale skin of his neck nicely. Mari took the package back into the bedroom. The cat was outside on the windowsill, looking in at Nanw. Mari put the present down on the bed and waited.

Their birthday ritual was set in stone: Dafydd would call and they'd spend the day together at the seaside. This was the start of summer for Mari: she couldn't for the life of her recall any summer before he was born. On a towel with her skirt turned up over her knees, Dafydd racing up and down after a swim... She had been afraid when they'd first started going, lonely as the beach was and knowing she would be useless as a lifeguard should any trouble arise. Her fear of the sea reduced her to jelly. But as he grew up, the beach became a second, sandy, salty home to Dafydd.

It was nearly dinnertime. He'd be here soon, bound to be. Mari made herself a bite to eat and fed Nanw. She made meat and salad rolls, tucking them into a nook of the basket on the kitchen table. She couldn't stop herself checking the clock.

She tidied up the letters, slipping some of them back into their envelopes. It was nearly two o'clock. At least they wouldn't be out in the hottest part of the day. There he'd be at the door as usual, and even though he was a young man now, he'd crinkle up his eyes in mischief like a little boy as they set off on the long path down to the sea, not bothering with small talk or any other wasted words. Mari started pottering around the house, did the washing up, sorted out some stuff in the boxes in the passageway. She thought about a job she had on: a necklace to repair, but really, he should be here by now. She went back out into the corridor and listened. Nothing. She went to sit on the bed again. It was nearly five o'clock. She stared at the packet lying on folds of bedclothes.

At the sound of footsteps, she jumped to her feet and rushed to the door, only calming down in time to open it.

"Mari?"

She recognised the girl straight away. Her hair was long and black; she looked as if she'd been crying.

"Yes?"

"I'm Catrin..." She paused.

"Oh, are you?" Mari didn't blink.

"Have you seen Dafydd?"

Mari's insides knotted when she heard his name.

"Dafydd?"

"Where is he?" The young woman looked around her as though some jack-in-the-box might spring out at her. "He told me he usually comes round here on his birthday... is he here?" Her posture was slack. Mari waited. "He's not answering the phone."

"Why don't you go over to his house then?" Mari asked smoothly.

The girl started to weep. "I... I... I've never been in his house! He wouldn't let me..."

79

Well, Dafydd wouldn't want his girlfriend seeing his mother in the state she was always in, would he? Mari's attitude softened.

"Come in." The young woman followed the older one obediently into the bedroom. "Sit down there. I'll get you some water."

The girl sat drying her tears on the sleeve of her jumper. By the time Mari got back from the kitchen, Catrin was holding hands with Nanw through the bars of the cage.

"Don't touch her! She bites." The girl took the glass in slender fingers. Mari sat on the bed and continued, "If you really knew him," she hesitated, "you'd know he does this sometimes... goes off to have a think about things. His dad was just the same."

"I didn't know his dad," Catrin murmured.

"No," Mari agreed, "not many people did."

The girl swallowed the water in scared sips.

"Is that for Dafydd?" Catrin had seen the present.

Mari hid the package behind her back.

"That's between me and him." Mari looked her up and down. "Doesn't look too promising if you haven't even been to his house yet, does it?" Her guts felt taut.

The girl looked down into her drink. Catrin started, "You know he told me," Mari turned to look at her, "that you thought we're too young..." Mari kept quite still. Nanw became agitated. "But I love him... He'll change his mind... I know he will." Mari's shoulders broadened. "He'll come back and everything'll be OK." Her young eyes were flinty.

The pair looked at each other for some time. Nanw had reached through the bars to grab a lock of the girl's black hair. Clever monkey! Catrin jumped up, screaming as Nanw tugged it, sending the water in a shower all over the floor. Mari made a show of scolding the monkey.

"I warned you!" The water darkened Catrin's clothes and she rubbed her scalp. Nanw was leaping up and down, laughing wildly, wires of the girl's hair wrapped around her fingers. Catrin looked from monkey to owner and turned on her heel.

"That monkey's crazy. You're not much better!"

Catrin rushed out. Mari followed a few paces behind but let her disappear down into the village. The sky was ripening towards night. Sighing happily, Mari glanced both ways before she shut the door. Nanw had calmed down. Mari slotted a nut between the bars and watched her snatch it up.

"That's it, sweetheart... that's it, lovely! Aren't you a good girl then?"

Whatever had happened to Dafydd? Mari fetched a candle from the mantelpiece, taking it over to the window. She struck a match. The flame waltzed admiringly with its own reflection. Mari went to sit on the bed once more, cuddling up into a blanket. She sat watching the flame through the darkness until it had absorbed all her fatigue. Dafydd must be out there in the world becoming a man all on his own. The light had cast a spell on Nanw but then the flame was stifled by its own wax, leaving the room quite black.

Chapter 19

Mari craned her neck up at the tall house one last time. No one had answered. It was a bright day; colourfully dressed tourists were smattered around the harbour. Children in macs, fishing with red buckets, made a rim of tangerine peel around the wall. Mari knocked again. She listened: no response. Time to go home, then.

"Mari!" Gwyn was standing at the fence. She stepped towards him.

"Gwyn, I'm sorry to…"

He came up the path with a heavy sack on his back.

"Not at all, I've been…"

"I can see you're busy."

"On the beach."

An awkward pause which sent Gwyn's eyes darting.

"I've brought the gemstones."

"I didn't think you'd get them so quickly."

"Well, I keep some stuff – a few little pieces – in the house for mending things."

"Oh, I see. Um, well you'd better come in."

"No… no, I don't want to bother you."

A thought occurred to Gwyn. "Cup of tea?" He left the sack at the foot of the steps and took a key out of his pocket. In case of flooding, sandbags had been left on each side of the door; the salty air had corroded its paint into miniature green curls. Gwyn picked up his sack again, leaving its impression a dark stain on the slate. "Come in."

Mari followed his lead along the passageway's zigzag of

tiles. The dark took some getting used to. Fishing rods were stacked around the banister's newel post, while from its knob hung a Barber jacket. A primrose cardigan was folded on the bottom step. Gwyn led her to the back of the house and into the narrow kitchen. The kettle was soon singing happily. He took out one of his best teacups. The table was a tangle of bills and papers; last year's calendar was nailed to the wall. Mari felt in her pocket for the plastic bag and squeezed the stones between her fingers. She took her tea and smiled at him.

"The little clock… I wanted the gemstones for the clock." Mari nodded as he sat down opposite her. The table was so small their knees were almost touching. "It's a watch, actually, but I thought with a proper case it'd make a nice grandfather clock for the house." His shyness receded. "I've been working on it since," he hesitated, "for months and months."

"Well," Mari said, "I've brought plenty to choose from."

"Would you like to see the house?" The idea brought life into Gwyn's features.

"Oh, I don't want to –" The life started to fade. "Well, why not?"

Gwyn got up, smoothing down his trousers over his knees. He swung his sack over his shoulder and they went upstairs. The carpet had worn away at the centre of the steps and the wallpaper – up towards the ceiling – had come loose. It seemed much darker by the time they reached the attic landing.

"I've closed off the other rooms." Gwyn took hold of a doorknob with one hand. "They're not much use to me now." Mari nodded. "I won't turn the light on… you should see it like it's supposed to be."

The pair went into the darkened room. The window had been boarded up, although a faint frame of light gave form to what were otherwise silhouettes around the floor. It was chilly in there. The sack took its place among the lumpen half-lit objects. It was a large square bedroom: probably once the best in the house. It was carpeted in beachcombings: driftwood, ropes and bits of iron, all lovingly licked into shape by the waves of the sea.

"Be careful," Gwyn said in a low voice, and Mari's stomach gave a lurch as he took her hand and pulled her gently over to a desk in one corner. The outline of a house shimmered in the gloom. His excitement was tangible.

"Stay there," he said, opening the roof. He folded out the front walls as though he were setting up a puppet theatre. His voice came closer to her ear. "Are you ready?"

"Yes, I am," Mari whispered.

Gwyn's hands were trembling but he managed to flick a switch somewhere in the darkness.

Amazing! The house was all light. Gwyn's eyes were twinkling. Mari stood staring in wonder at every little room with its polished chairs and plush carpets, each one a work of art. The silk wallpaper lining every wall gave off a blush of pinks and crimson. The armchairs were draped with cosy blankets and underneath each bed was a tiny pair of slippers waiting for their master. There was even a music room with a violin leaning on a chair, and a piano – complete with miniature vase and bouquet – ready for the maestro to sit down and strike up a polka. A mirror hung above each fireplace. In the living room, the dresser shelves were laden with willow-pattern plates, while its hooks – neat as ear-rings – dangled little jugs. Snuggled up to the fire were two chairs, with a cat curled up on one of its cushions. Mari could happily step into that world this very minute! As she lingered over every gorgeous detail, Gwyn turned to her with a smile.

"It's perfect, isn't it?"

The house spotlights were up and held the pair in a kindly soft focus.

"Yes, perfect!"

Chapter 20

When would Dafydd come home? Mari had cut up apple chunks for Nanw, who hadn't been eating properly. She was feeding them through the bars in an attempt to tempt her. The monkey just sat there in a hunched-up sulk, accepting the pieces only to bat them back and leave them on the cage floor so that they rotted in the warm air. Frowning, Mari decided to let her stew in her own juices while she was out with Mo. She went to get washed, using cold water and holding the flannel to her forehead so long that it began to absorb the heat from her skin. She put on a short-sleeved blouse and a skirt without a petticoat.

Mo had asked her to come along with her to a storage unit on the outskirts of town. She hadn't found a buyer yet for the stock she wasn't keeping and hoped to store it there in the meantime. Her bungalow was fit to burst, she'd said, the children's rooms packed with junk ever since they'd flown the nest. Hardly room to swing a kitten, so that when the grandkids came for a sleepover they'd have to bunk down on the sofa or the floor. This was Mo's roundabout way of telling Mari that soon she would be giving up the market.

Even though the car windows were open and both women's arms were bare, the heat stopped their usual chatter. Listening to the wind tickling the leaves in the hedgerows, they fell into an uneasy reverie. Sweat was making Mo's spectacles constantly slip down her nose.

The storage unit was huge and unremarkable, just like all the other buildings sprung up overnight on this scruffy scrap of land skirting the town. In the little office at the entrance was a man managing to read the newspaper despite his proximity to a noisy fan. He looked up and Mo smiled at him.

"Can I have a look at one of your rooms, please?" she said.

"God, I'm cooking in here!" He turned off the fan so they could both hear properly. He gave Mo a densely typed leaflet. "It's all in there. You're not allowed anything dangerous... No petrol or flammable stuff; no food or anything that might go off, either. I'll be keeping an eye out. Sundays are busy; try not to come then. Most people come at the weekend." He tapped his nose. "It's pretty quiet the rest of the week: one or two regulars, but to be honest, hardly anyone else. Pick up the key from me and bring it back after. The prices are all down there." He had the speech off by heart; his eyes were already creeping back to the newsprint. He gave Mo the key. "Have a look at the room – it's over there." He thumbed backwards.

"Heavens!" The women were laughing by the time they came out of the office.

They walked into the heart of the place: it was as tall as a cathedral. They moved closer together as the fan recommenced, signalling they were on their own. The floors were smooth and clean. The cool of such a large building was a salve on Mari's skin; only their footsteps broke the holy hush. Cut open, the place would display a man-made honeycomb of identical cells connected by corridors. Hundreds of doors, each decorated with a metal lock to keep valuables in and vandals out.

"It says 545 on the key," Mo whispered.

Mari started looking at the numbers painted above each long row. The heat was making Mo pant slightly.

Out here where no one lived, people brought those things that had once been a part of their lives. All that they didn't need any more they cradled in their arms, dumped in a little cage and turned a key on it, like pushing a nagging memory to the back of your mind. At times, the transaction would only be short-lived. At others, it would be forever. Houses are too small to hold all the stuff we've started acquiring. Some of it inherited a while ago; some we no longer even recognise: but all surplus to requirements. Our lives are too busy, too full for us to face the mess we've made and put our house in order. People hooked on shopping have to turn for space and perspective to these cloisters.

From open doors along the aisle came the telltale sounds of someone spending time inside their cell. Maybe moving an item from left to right; taking a trip down memory lane; possibly adding to the pile but failing to disturb the layers underneath. If you lived in town, this might be the only quiet spot you had. They saw boxes in a row with a man in a sleeping bag squeezed between them, making the most of the peace to catch up on his reading. Mo sped up, pulling Mari after her. The corridor was cut away once more to reveal a woman writing at a desk in a robber's cave of treasure. She looked up and smiled at them.

The couple reached 545 and unlocked it, opening the heavy door with difficulty. They went inside a small, dry room built of grey bricks.

"Wouldn't fancy being locked in here," Mo's whisper bounced off the walls.

"Must be how Nanw feels!" Mari joked. "Is it big enough for you?"

Mo concurred, her breath a rasp. "It won't be for long." She paused to inhale. "Don't like this place. Hems you in, doesn't it? Dai can bring our stuff over." Mo glanced around her. "Time's come to say goodbye to the market." Because Mo had been so worried about Mari, she hadn't realised how much she would miss it herself. "But this... this is a sad old dump, isn't it?" Mo looked serious for once. "All lined up like egg boxes but every room packed to the rafters with rubbish!"

For the first time in weeks, Mari longed to be out in the heat of the sun. "Things'll get better," she said. Wasn't this what Gwyn had told her?

"We had some good times at the market, didn't we?"

"Yes. Come on," Mari replied, taking Mo over to the door.

"It's all a cycle," Mo said, reflective for the first time in a while. "We clear out the houses. Things move on. A clean slate to set up home all over again – that's what couples want." She looked at Mari. "But there's something unnatural about this place, isn't there?"

Mari eventually managed to budge Mo; they manhandled the door back into position and felt the release of escape.

"It'll be Dai's job to bring our things here."

Mari clasped Mo's arm. "Let's go and get chips, shall we? On the front – and a ninety-nine?"

"Yes!" Mo cheered up. "Haven't had one of those in ages."

The man looked up briefly from his paper to take the key back and jot down Mo's name by Room 545. Mari took a deep breath. Both women felt a little more lively in the warm sunshine, but Mo kept a tight hold on Mari's arm all the same.

Chapter 21

Mari opened the door. He seemed a changed man, his cheekbones razor sharp despite their obvious lack of recent contact with a shaver. There was a pink crescent of a scar on his eyelid. His beach towel was slung over his shoulder.

"Ready, then?" Dafydd asked. Mari didn't reply. "Come on, I reckon it's warm enough."

"All that food's gone to waste."

"Come on... We always go to the beach."

Mari found herself relenting.

It was an unseasonable scorcher. The shrubs were abuzz with bees; the horizon was a smudge of sea mist.

"Where've you been?"

Dafydd leaned on the doorjamb. "Needed time to think... but everything's sorted now."

Mari looked him up and down. "I'll just get my things."

His smile spread like a picnic rug flung out for a feast.

The prospect of a cliff-path walk in this heat had put off all other comers. The pair had first choice, picking their usual spot halfway along, far back from the sea, where the sand met marram grass. Mari found a flat patch on which to set up camp. She sat on her towel, bare-shouldered in a camisole top, her skirt folded up over her knees. Dafydd pulled his shirt over his head. His arms and legs were dappled with bruises. Sara must still be up to her old tricks, then...

His towel was spread out beside hers. Underneath his trousers, he already had his trunks on, showing how sure he'd been that Mari would be won over. He took off his T-shirt and his shoes.

"Be back in a bit," he said with a cheeky grin, picking his way easily across the pebbles then gearing up for a sprint towards the sea.

"Be care —"

He wouldn't hear her warning through the waves anyway.

The sea was pleased with herself today, serene in azure silk with a mermaid's tail of snowy frills sashaying to and fro. Dafydd dived into her arms. Hidden grasshoppers had set up a vocal protest about the heat. A few lazy, light blue butterflies were in camouflage against the harebells growing at the cliff base. The ocean's constant twitching for attention made her so sick she couldn't settle either until Dafydd returned safely. His pale head was a pearl against the blue. Mari would never be a swimmer. She couldn't trust the sea: it was worse than two-faced, reaching for a fresh-coloured mask each time the sky clouded over or when surprised by its own dipping depths. Her worst dreams were filled with its swishing sounds. Trying to get out, Dafydd briefly lost his balance but he shook off the water's embrace, finding a careful footing on the sharp shells. He wrapped his towel tightly around his waist and settled down with his back to Mari. They sat listening to the waves with the wind on their faces.

"How's your mother?" Mari asked in a low voice.

"She's OK." His words were almost carried away on the breeze but they grew in power when he added, "It'll all be all right now. I've been thinking... I'm going to sell the business – what's left of it – and go travelling. Want to see the world. Then Mam'll have to stand on her own two feet." His hair was slick. The sea was a seductive whisper in the distance. Mari let him get it all off his chest. "Me and Catrin've split up. I've been trying to phone her but she won't answer.

There's nothing to keep me here now." Mari's skin came up in goose pimples. A droplet of water was forming, caught in a curl of hair at his nape.

"Oh," she said.

The sun was drying his skin. Mari thought about Nanw pulling that healthy lock of Catrin's hair. Defeat had been on her face as she left the house, even though she'd sounded defiant.

"What was *your* mother like?"

This was not an easy question for Mari to answer.

"Don't remember much, really."

"Same as me with Dat."

"Yes, something like that. I know she was pretty... really pretty." Mari leaned back on her arms, choosing best-suited words. The sun was almost at its highest point. "Hair black as a raven... porcelain skin... green eyes that lit up when she laughed. So kind, too; not like Father. Always smart in a skirt and lipstick. She left me lipstick kisses on my cheek!" Dafydd smiled, imagining such an ideal mother. "She wore perfume, too, always the same, and she'd read me stories – just like I did with you."

"I remember..."

"I did my best for you..."

"I know."

Mari's smile faded. "But Father was," she struggled, "different."

"I can't remember Dat..."

"Mine was nothing like your father." She paused. "Your dad was big like you but soft as a feather." The drop of saltwater was swelling, clinging for life onto its hook of yellow hair. "He was strong but fair. People thought we were brother and sister, y'see? Two peas in a pod: the same way of looking at the world, the same way of moving..." Mari could see the muscles in Dafydd's shoulder tightening. Her speech had slowed right down. "He was just like a brother to me."

Whether this was the right moment, Mari couldn't be sure, but she rummaged in her bag anyway, taking out the little oblong box. Without asking him to turn around, she balanced the box on his shoulder. He reached back to fetch it and bent his head to open its contents, setting the box aside. Her pulse was racing. She heard a clink when he passed the chunky chain back over his shoulder. She cupped it and shuffled closer behind him, the links curled up in her palm. She uncoiled the gold cord so that the sun caught it in a maternal caress. She closed the clasp around his neck, brushing the baby-soft skin at his nape. It looked perfect. Dafydd touched it lightly with his fingers. All through this exchange, neither had spoken until he said quietly, "Thanks."

The lock of hair, now lower than the necklace, released the droplet to send it bowling down the boy's backbone, snapping back up into a tight curl after the weight was lifted. Dafydd's shoulders were muscled and his flesh was hot. He shifted his buttocks. The tide spewed the waves across the sand towards Mari. The droplet was playing a game of stop-start, leaving behind it a snail's trail of sheen. Mari gazed at its teardrop shape. The salty teardrop couldn't stick to its course: its true path down the centre of his back had been diverted so that now it was plying the warm rungs of Dafydd's ribs.

Mari was starting to feel uncomfortably warm. They had pushed their ritual rather late into the season: she wasn't used to this ripe sun, hot and proud in its prime. Dafydd's skin was going red; his back crystalised with specks of salt. He knew she was watching him, all right. The shiny little pearl had thought the better of straying too far and had gone back to the middle of his back before slipping suddenly to the base of his spine. The seagulls were screeching.

"Oh, it's too hot for me here..." Dafydd got up and ran over to the waves without a glance over his shoulder. Mari realised that his back had been turned to her all this while. You couldn't see his feet for sand rising. A pair of butterflies went dancing past. They moved together as though attached by an invisible thread: one swooped back and the other couldn't help but follow.

Chapter 22

Nanw hadn't slept for nights on end. Her skin was like parchment and her eyes were wild. Mari had decided to stay at home to look after her, and for once the monkey didn't resent the change in her routine, laid out as she was in her cage with one arm flopped between the bars. Mari was sure she had a fever, made worse by the unnaturally close weather. Mari had opened the windows and she'd been bathing her in cold wet flannels, but Nanw still stayed torpid, her eyes in pearly stillness now, robbed of their usual mischief. Wait for the temperature to fall: that was all she could do. She peeled off the damp swaddling that had taken on the small body's heat, plunging it back into cold water. Nanw was shivering as Mari wrung it out with hands ringed red, and rearranged it across the monkey's back. She'd be better once she'd rested. In such a small frame, a fever was usually short-lived.

The door was wide open, letting the wind in to play among the dresses that were still hanging there. Dafydd had come home after their day at the seaside and gone to sit in the best room where she was sitting now, since it was coolest. Mari gave in to temptation and opened the toy box to take another look at the emerald. It was already incredibly lovely. She'd burnished some of its faces so that from its hearthstone flared a fire of colour. She may as well do a little work while Nanw was napping. Mari's throat was tight as she adjusted the jewel on the wheel; nothing must be out of synch. The emerald was shaping up: excitement stirred as she settled to work. Mari was aiming for the classic emerald cut. Some jewellers went for a flashier multi-faceted affair but to her mind the traditional one, with its long smooth face, showed up the gem's colour best. At present the fingerprint was smudged at the stone's centre so that you could only see it when the light slanted in a certain way. Her job now was to shape the base so that light was directed through the inclusion. Mari was a bundle of nerves.

She cut, she polished, she stuck to it until each surface was perfect. Nothing should obscure the light's journey through the gemstone. She tipped it, working at all angles to avoid any mistake. This was the most important stone she'd cut, as well as the most expensive. She'd bought it cheaply, most likely because the owner had doubted she could turn it into a valuable jewel. It was warm under her fingertips; she knew every surface like the back of her hand. Mari looked into its interior. The fingerprint too she now knew intimately. The final cuts were so difficult, but Mari felt a great peace as she sensed perfection approaching. The shadow of the cat stalked along the wall and into the bedroom where Nanw was.

At dinnertime Mari got up and stretched, then went into the kitchen to make herself cheese on toast. The lawn and shrubs were turning brown in the terrible heat. A few birds were in the branches, beaks open, gawping at the sun. She drank some tea and went back to work.

She sat down and held up the emerald against the natural light. The scintillating stone threw a green shadow along her face. Mari heard a noise and turned to see Nanw out of the cage and standing in the doorway, eyeing up Mari and the jewel. The green of the emerald flashed in the monkey's eyes. The stone slipped through Mari's fingers and onto her lap. She screamed and hid her mouth. Nanw's teeth were sunk deep into the cat's neck and its body hung lifeless from the monkey's jaw, blood dripping onto the lino. Nanw looked up at Mari sitting there, appalled but unable to move. The beast was breathing fiercely and her eyes were dancing.

Chapter 23

Mari buried the cat at the bottom of the garden. The soil was baked hard into red dust. She had bought a new lock for the cage and would keep Nanw in there from now on. The monkey still had a temperature. Hopefully that would explain why she'd made that attack. Still though, the time had come to stop treating her like a child.

Nanw had started to stalk onto the stage of her dreams, an eye-rolling beast whose histrionics upended the most insipid masque into nightmare pantomime. Nanw hamming up a raid on the toy box for the emerald, which she promptly swallowed. Nanw throwing huge shadows as she crept, obviously, along the corridor, on her way to snatch the jewel and snuff it out on the hearthstone. Mari was forced to watch this dumbshow with her own mouth gagged before she woke up in a sweat. The real monkey, shrunk to doll size, slept on, while Mari stared at the ceiling until dawn.

She had been off work so long it felt like a practice run for when the market finally closed. Until Nanw was well again, Mari was as trapped as the creature. In order to kill time, she took out the quiet man's last letters, trying to decipher the wavering lines of blue. Reading his thoughts was like doing a jigsaw when someone had hidden the lid. Even so, she should be able to form a full picture of him, once all the wobbly scraps were to hand and committed to memory.

Mari was lying on the bed, puzzling, when she heard the sound of familiar footsteps. Opening her eyes, she smiled and went over to the door.

"Why didn't you say Catrin had been here?" His face was angry and sweating from the exertion of a fast walk up from the village. Mari turned back inside to sit on the bed. "Tell me!"

"She *was* here," Mari admitted. Dafydd was pacing up and down but Nanw didn't even notice. His eyes were darting to and fro, chasing conflicting thoughts. "I didn't think it was important." Mari blushed.

"Didn't think it *important*?" Dafydd went right up to her.

"But you said she didn't matter..."

"You can read my mind, can you?"

Mari straightened up. "You said you'd thought about it and you'd decided... I didn't want to bother you since you were so sure. You can't say I don't know you, Dafydd."

"Why've you always got to interfere in my life?"

"I was doing what was best for you... so you'd get a chance to do things. Things I never could."

"What? 'Doing what was best'?" Dafydd's hands were shaking and he'd raised his voice. "If you'd really wanted what was best for me, you'd have left my dad well alone! Mam told me I couldn't trust you!" Mari turned her back on him but his words were echoing. He grew calmer. Outrage shot up through Mari's body like mercury. "Mari, please, I didn't mean..." The young man was sitting by the cage, Nanw bedridden beside him. "Catrin's gone." His voice was softer. "Her flat's empty; she's left no number, nothing..."

Dafydd pressed his palm hard against his forehead and started weeping.

Mari listened without offering comfort. "You can think whatever you like," she said quietly, "but I wanted whatever was best for you, Dafydd." She swivelled round to face him. His arms were thinner than when she'd last seen him. "And that's all I wanted for your dad too." Dafydd hardly suppressed a laugh and shook his head. The air in the room was oppressive. "You'd better go now." Mari's voice was steely.

Dafydd got up, his eyes glowing like coals. He stuck his nose right into her face and spat, "What's *important* is always what *you* want, isn't it?" Their eyes met. "The hell with everybody else... Mam calls you an old witch, and that's what you are!" His voice was so strained that Nanw had looked up and started to sob. Mari managed to control her temper and keep quiet. "I'll never forgive you for what you did to Dat."

Mari gave a start when the door banged. She kept the tears at bay and stayed on the bed, hands locked together. Those last letters and their envelopes were interleaved, like lovers. She picked up the most recent page to try and keep her mind occupied. The heat bore down on her, leaving her limp. She sought for signs among squiggles of ink italics, but any meaning had gone missing. The blue lines had been cut off in crucial places so that the scrambled sentences made no sense. Mari had hoped that by now a photofit of the dead man might have ghosted across the paper, shadows of a soul in silver halide. A real person she could treasure in her breast pocket. But Mari found the page empty: just a jumble of things he'd jotted down throughout his life, mistaking ink for immortality. Scrunching the letter in her fist, she threw it into the grate for next winter's kindling.

Nanw did not hear Mari weeping steadily in her bed that night.

Chapter 24

Mari woke up early in a swelter, the hair at her temples damp. She had been dreaming about the quiet man and the girl on the bike: a happy biopic in glorious technicolour. Now, all she could see ahead of her were bright lights in an inconstant, twisting column of colour. She strained her head up to look at her hands, but she couldn't see them. She'd stay blind like this until all feeling in her fingers and mouth was lost; then the headache would start. This would squeeze every nerve of her brain and leave her in terror of the next contraction. It was a waiting game. She couldn't get comfortable on either side of the bed.

She thought of Dafydd as she watched the lightning in her internal storm. It was only a few hours since she'd seen him but it might as well have been centuries. She had spent years in fear of hearing those words and now here they were, oscillating in her eardrum like tinnitus. It was almost a relief for them to be out in the open. The aura was swaying about now like searchlights over an ocean liner, one which had taken her stomach with it on its churning passage. Nanw was chuntering to herself.

Mari turned and lay down again. Now her view was from the deck, up into a starry night sky. In more ways than one, Dafydd was her baby, and she had nearly lost him once already when his mother had managed to poison him against Mari. She couldn't face losing him again... The best thing would be just to give him time to think it over. He was his father's son, after all. He'd see sense in the long run.

She had pins and needles in her fingertips. The little punctures made their way up her arms and into her face. By the time they reached her mouth, it felt as though her body had been trapped under a relentless tattooist's needle. Her tongue was a flap of leather: she couldn't swallow, so she turned onto her side to let the drool dribble onto the pillow. She lay still, feeling nothing whatsoever. Mari relaxed. Her body was frozen. With a crooked smile, she let herself enjoy the feeling for a moment. She closed her eyes to watch the firework show. No pleasure without pain. The latter was primed for action in the wings.

The fuzzy shapes faded and pain pricked in their stead. It took its time: it always did. A little black seed had been planted in her mind, long ago, and in the right conditions it would grow and grow until it swallowed her, body and soul. It would start behind her eyes and spread like fire through her head. The pain gathered strength, returning to her hands. Her body timed how long it stayed numb, as though it were conspiring against her, to make her start feeling again just when the pain was at its peak.

On becoming a woman – when she'd first begun to bleed – that was when the headaches had started. Every month she would be in the bathroom swilling out flannel cloths, finding it impossible to tell her father. Other girls would go on a special trip to town with their mothers for a pep talk and essential purchases. All she'd got was Miss Jones coming over for a chat and swearing her to secrecy! Father had other things to think about and anyway, he was under the weather himself; surely she could see that.

Mari traced her own face, like a blind woman seeing the shape of her own nose, the softness of skin gone a little slack around the mouth, her skull solid within.

Pain slithered into her like snakes in the dark, frightening

106

thought out of the room. Outside it was getting hot and muggy, real lightning this time forking the horizon. No pill could help her... Might as well... Mari reached for the cord of her dressing gown and tied it tightly around her forehead. Her face was twisted. She tried to sit up and managed to pull off her nightie. Her head felt as though it were Pandora's box, the sins of the world, its curses, fighting to be let out. The sky lit up once more, sending flashes of grey along her naked body.

As a teenager she'd had a migraine every week. She'd miss school, have to stay at home with somebody looking after her. She'd have the strangest dreams then too, but soon learned not to share them.

More recently she would know a bad spell was on its way whenever she could smell things more strongly or when colours seemed brighter. Her sense of taste would be enhanced too, and she'd get a sore throat. Even though she didn't have them so often now, each one was worse than the last, leaving Mari a piece of prey in the migraine's maw. She turned over again, seeking respite, but the pain stuck fast. She laid herself back out. Once, she got right out of bed, touching the floor with her tiptoes but thought better of it in case she should fall. She ground her teeth and pulled the cord tighter to give herself something else to think about. The blood surging through her cheeks pinched every nerve, sending currents of electricity along her neck. She held her head in her hands and pressed down hard.

Mo was used to Mari's bad spells. Whenever she went blind, Mo would lead her to her car and take her home, no questions asked. She'd put her to bed and close the door behind her, knowing Mari couldn't stand anyone being around her just then. Mari couldn't make up her mind which position was best, back or side. Her whole body was shivering, the whites of her eyes matched by the light of the moon, though the clouds threatened to eclipse it. The sea was black. She lay there for hours, dark veins throbbing, twisting around the idlest thought of Dafydd and deforming it.

At last the black-gloved hand loosened its grip, plopping Mari aside like an empty puppet. Keeping her eyelids shut, she plucked at the noose's slip-knot with one finger. Her eyes were darkly ringed. She had given up the fight: there was no strength left in her. Her arms and pulse were weak; she could hardly breathe. What was the point in struggling? The spite of her latest headaches had proven that a faceless enemy was the hardest to beat. Nature must run its course... A tear coursed down her cheek, which was a touch cooler now. If only she could have faith that this suffering would pass, she need no longer be afraid of these darkest hours before dawn. She would once more be able to sleep at night. Her hands were curled above her brows, making archways that offered cool in a bleached-out courtyard. Her eyes were so tired, her fingers blurred to a soft pink lattice and she fell forward into that blanking tunnel.

Nanw opened her eyes just as Mari closed hers. Mari's body at last was flung open, her throat like the fine curve of a china teacup, luminous in the half-light. The monkey shunted on her back to get closer to the single bed, stretching her arm out through the cage bars. She saw the gentle tremor of Mari's eyelids and extended one bony digit with its blackened talons in a bid to scrape at Mari's exposed neck.

Chapter 25

Leaning on a brush, Mari looked down towards the bay. The sunlight was harsh on her greyish skin, making her flinch when it struck her full in the face. She was frail and light of frame: she wouldn't go back to work until she was fully well. Mo had been calling like clockwork, fetching armfuls of merchandise, meantime, to sell on her friend's behalf. Mari spent the days inside tidying up or outside in the shadow cast by the cottage. By next spring she'd need to give the walls a new coat of whitewash, since the present one had been scoured by salt winds to a raddled off-white.

After dinner, Mari tucked one of her lighter blouses into her skirt: how easily her whole hand could slide inside her waistband now! She'd have to wash some clothes too: this long summer was stretching her wardrobe to its limits. She tied a headscarf around her forehead to shade her eyes, and stepped out into the sunshine.

Out on the calm sea, bright boats were pinned like specimens under glass. Families were making the most of their last days of holiday. She set off without really knowing where she was going. She took the winding road down towards the village, which seemed partly cut off from the shore by heat haze billowing its way along the coast. Mari felt that heat sapping her. Harebells twitched in the hedgerows as the breeze touched them, keeping their best features chastely tucked away under their caps. The scruffy heads of cornflower were a coarser blue. She loved these flowers. When she was a little girl she'd stuff them in jars and set herself down to draw among the fragrant foam of bloom. She still had a whole box of her best efforts somewhere. Mari stopped and chucked one of the harebells under its little light blue chin. Its petals were so terribly fragile that the slightest draught sent them tinkling. It was prettiness itself but she'd given up picking wildflowers once she'd realised how quickly they wilted.

There were so many tourists in the village, it was hard to find a friendly face. Mari started walking, her gaze fixed forwards. That headscarf made her feel – for a moment – as though she were some freewheeling fifties filmstar... She found herself taking the narrow old coastal path back out into the countryside. Low bushes and thorn sprawled in her way but the path had been kept open by determined sheep prepared to sacrifice a few tufts in the process. The sun was blazing down.

She went as far as the little gate below the cemetery and leant her hand on it. The place was in silence. Stepping onto the lawn, she disturbed a lizard sunbathing on a grave. Mari bent over the tap, cupped her hands and drank. The water was cold and clear. She splashed a little onto her face and in an instant it was dry.

Dafydd's father rested a way away, an arm of bramble pointing its spiky finger at his inscription. She didn't go over, even though the beech bouquet she'd left last time had dried to twigs, the odd brown leaf clinging on for life. She wasn't in the mood to talk. At the bottom, a red cloud was rising as three men cut a new grave. One raised a palm in greeting, showing rusty dust scored into sweat. Mari walked upwards, short of the church itself, where a shady area outside was reserved for clergy.

She hadn't been to this part of the cemetery since Father's funeral. It was in the best position, sheltered by the church and a green canopy of leaves which shifted like beseeching hands. His grave was close to the church porch, set apart from the other bodies by a low oblong wall. At least there were no separate bedrooms under the earth. The grass had been left to grow longer here. His grateful parish had paid for a memorial for him in blotched pink marble. Ivy was creeping along it now, though.

Having bequeathed his assets to the school and church, her father's good name was assured. Before that, he'd sat on every committee going, attended all the meetings. He visited the sick and prayed for those in attendance at their deathbed. Charging himself with chasing every last penny towards the church's support, he would spend days ensconced in his panelled study. Presiding as he did over so many weddings and baptisms, the community circled around his planet. So did she, but she had been one of many. She'd have been happy had he been a rock for her alone. Mari leaned on him, just like the others, but only added to his load. He had been her life. He'd tried diverting her ardour to loftier heroes. But an ordinary father's love would have been enough. He'd been kind to so many people, impatient with others, even cruel to a few. He was only a man, after all.

For the first time ever, Mari stepped over the low wall and stood at his grave. Had any tears come, they would have fast evaporated in the warm air. The whole place was dry, the grass a whisper of cricket-song, the ground singeing to brown. Then she broke the spell and walked off. Well away from that walled enclosure, she stood in the light and shed her burden. She made her way back onto the path. Having seen the grave now, she decided that she would never go there again. It was all over.

She had reached the far end of the graveyard. Her headache had abated and her eyes adjusted at last to the bright light. She took off her headscarf and waved it like a proud flag of surrender. She listened to children laughing as they played on the beach below. Mari smiled. She had things to get on with: finish that emerald; sort out how to earn a living. And she had to go and see Gwyn. Mari opened the gate, went through it and without looking back once, she shut it behind her.

Chapter 26

All night long, Mari had been working on the jewel. She'd finished it in the darkest hours, before the break of day. An imaginary bugle sounding in her head, she had plucked it off the metal spike and wiped it under the desk-lamp. Putting it on the palm of her hand, she'd examined it in the bright glare. Radiance racketed against those reflecting walls until it burst out in a blaze of green flame. The emerald had eradicated all doubt from Mari's mind: her faith in it was complete. She trusted it to tell the truth. Mari wiped away a tear and turned it in the light to watch the fingerprint glowing gold.

Dawn licked its balm across the landscape as Mari went to wake up Nanw. Her health was failing steadily despite Mari's tender care. She'd been forced out a couple of times to fetch food, but every trip had been curtailed by a sense of duty. The monkey's temper had cooled to an un-Nanw-like mood of mildness. Mari opened the cage and drew the animal onto her lap then onto the bed, trying to get the monkey to sit beside her and supporting her back the way you'd help an infant.

"Here we are... Look!"

In front of Nanw's lean face, Mari's hand had opened like a flower: at its stamen, the green stone. The monkey's tired eyelids opened to stare at it. The jewel beamed back at the gentle new sun. It had certainly entranced Nanw: the monkey reached out slowly and Mari let the dark little fingers fondle the bright droplet. She pressed her cheek against the monkey's and the pair waltzed together on that soft green lawn. Tired of it now, Nanw drew back her hand and closed her eyes on the show. Mari kissed the sleeping monkey on the head and put her back into the cage, laying her across a small bath of lukewarm water. Having closed the door firmly, she stayed close by, only realising, when she noticed the clock, that Mo would be coming round soon.

Since today was a quiet one for the market, the pair planned to look at a house in town. Mari wanted to get out for a while and, by the look of things, all Nanw needed was to sleep. Mari slipped the emerald back into its rag and into her pocket, to show Mo later.

Summer was now past its prime: the coast had been subjected to endless aching weeks of sunshine. Electricity was crackling in the air; the blanking light made the trees stand out sharply. The clouds had been churned into a grey mass, audibly choking the sky. Every rumble made Nanw cringe. Mari tucked a mac into her bag and waited for Mo on the doorstep in the heat. Her thin blouse did little to mop up the stream of sweat down her back. Signs of autumn were in the hedgerows, along with rattling browning leaves.

The house was just outside town, four-square in a lovely garden that had run wild. The pair took the path around the back. The house had been built between the wars, with large windows in every direction to catch the light. Mo wiped the damp from her face with a handkerchief then opened the door. Inside was a mess: stuff all over the place and the kitchen smothered. They'd be at it for days. Mo had rolled up her sleeves but the sweat was glowing on her cheeks and her breathing rattled. The heat was playing havoc with her lungs.

"We'll do the biggest stuff today. Dai and me'll come back to sort the rubbish."

Mari nodded.

The walls were a pinkish cream, while the furniture – like the house – dated from the thirties. The table in the modest kitchen was plain wood. Tea towels, thick with dust, were folded over the oven handle. The living room looked out to the sea. Mo started marking up furniture as Mari sat on the wide windowsill and admired the view. Seagulls drifted, like dandruff, towards shoulders of landscape. The cloud mass had swollen like an injured limb about to leak its fluids. She could hear Mo riffling through the other rooms but Mari was happy to do nothing. She'd been reading the quiet man's letters for weeks now without being any the wiser: for the first time in years her appetite for prying into other people's papers was sated. She took a cushion from one of the armchairs and leaned back against the wall to wait. Mo had started up her usual whistling. The heat was stifling as Mari watched the sky lour and then finally release daubs of warm rain against the window. The heat broke like a delicate teacup, sending electric filigrees down to the sea. The room was lit like a stage. The wind got up, then claps of thunder drew Mo back in there. She sat in the window with Mari.

"God's throwing furniture around again," Mo muttered.

The horizon sparked as though it were a live wire. Its throat too dry to swallow the rain, the earth let it drool off in rivulets through the dust. Before long, a flood was flowing down the road in front of the house. Mo caught Mari's eye and they started counting the distance between flashes and thunderclaps, smiling each time the rip-roaring sky stopped their "One, two, three". Mari worried about how Nanw was faring.

The waves were whipping up white horses onto the shore. The sea was heaving back and forth, splashing against the land so you couldn't see where one started and the other ended. Mo got up and went to fetch the food basket. She poured out a cup each for them from the flask, refreshment for while the entertainment lasted.

"That's cleared the air!" she said, looking out to sea and then glancing at Mari, who seemed in a trance. "Are you OK?"

Mari turned to Mo, smiling at her. "Yes."

"You look a bit different, that's all."

Mari took the emerald out of her pocket and placed it on Mo's palm. The lightning flashed around the room but it was pleasure that lit up Mo's face.

"You did it!" Mo put down her cup. Her eyes were almost eating the emerald up. "It's... it's just lovely!" Mari was so pleased. "Got an even stronger battery than this storm!" She gave it back to Mari with a smile. "I knew you'd do it sooner or later."

The pair settled down to watch the old season's death pangs.

By the time they'd finished their tea, the thunder was taking longer to respond to the lightning's provocation, the raindrops were less insistent that they be let in, and the clouds had cried themselves dry.

Well, if this wasn't the most handsome house she had ever seen... Walking to Mo's car, fingers curled lightly around the emerald in her pocket, Mari's nostrils were filled with the sweet smell of clean earth.

Chapter 27

Mari opened the windows onto a fresher morning. The sky was a deep blue, ragged after the storm's crisis. Terrified of the thunder, Nanw had been sick all over her bedclothes so that they'd had to be washed and hung out to dry. She looked a little better now, though; perhaps the fever had passed. Mari had tried to tempt her by popping a nut and then some meat into her mouth, but each morsel had plopped out uneaten from slack lips. Mari had gone to sort out the jewellery, trying to decide whether a ring or a necklace would best suit the emerald. She was tidying up at the back of the house when Mo arrived and went straight to Mari's bedroom to sit by Nanw's cage. Back Mari came into the room, and –

"Mo!" Mo was white as a bedsheet. She was cradling a box and looked Mari in the eye. "What's wrong?" Mari asked. Mo looked down, almost panting. "You'd better use your inhaler," Mari pleaded. "Your chest…" Mo shook her head. "Mo, tell me!"

Mo held the black box out to her. Her voice was lifeless like an invalid's.

"I've found… what you've been looking for," she said, starting to cry. Mari looked at her in fear. Mo recovered a little and they held each other's gaze. "I've got what you were looking –" Mo repeated. "Brought them over soon as I could." Mo couldn't stop trembling as she tipped up the sides to show Mari its contents. "I couldn't sleep so I went back to the house…"

"Which house?"

"Where we were yesterday… you know!" Mari tried her

best to follow her friend's words. "Please." Mari looked at the box, her eyes slightly sunken. Her fingers, pulled back against her chest, were plaited flat as though in a prayer gone wrong. "Please, love." Mari reached her arms out slowly to take it, bringing a dark shadow across her pale face. She stepped back and sat with it on the bed. Mo's eyes were pinned on Mari. The dark oblong sat impassive under Mari's palm while one tear fell and wet its lid. She wiped the droplet but it stayed put, staining the cardboard blacker. "Leave it if you can't..." Mo admitted defeat, kneeling at Mari's feet. She leaned forward to hold her companion's arm.

"It's just – I've waited so long!" Mari gasped.

"S... sorry it was me that found them."

Mari smiled sadly.

"I was ready to give up... Well, nearly, anyway. I... I didn't look at all when we were in there, you know? Maybe it wasn't me who was meant to find them." Mo was biting her fingernails raw.

"D'you want me to go?" Mari shook her head and slid a hand across the lid. "I was clearing under the bed," Mo went on. "I'd brought lamps with me... It was three in the morning and I just came across it..."

"Under the bed?"

Mo nodded. After all these years, how could Mari baulk at bringing it into the light? A chapter in her life was over.

"Come on," Mo whispered as she squeezed her arm gently. "Come on, open it."

Her heart was doing somersaults but she tucked her fingers under the lid and flipped it open. News clippings yellow with age and folded together in paper nests. They were in a different order, but they were an exact match for the ones Mari had in her identical hidey-hole. A neat date on each was marked in her mother's hand. A tear blurred the ink's precision.

A photo of a baby. A baby in a nurse's arms. Left on the vicar's doorstep. Oh Lord, sweet Lord...

Although she knew the story off by heart, she read it again. Evidence of hypothermia; some degree of malnutrition. Any possible witnesses will have last seen the infant wearing a white gown sometime in the early hours. Mari looked at her own face in miniature, eyes closed against the flash of cameras and the weight of weeping. Police appeals for a young woman behaving out of the ordinary, or a married woman no one had seen for a while. *No response from the public.* "It's a miracle," *the vicar said. He had been up at prayer when he heard the baby crying.* "A little girl as a gift." *A little girl come out of the mist.* "She will be welcome in my home." *Police concern in connection with the mother's health.* Mari shut the box. Mo was still kneeling down.

"She kept them!" Mari sobbed. Neither of them had heard Nanw getting up feebly to press her face against the cage bars. "As long as I'd no proof, I had hope." Her voice was thick with emotion. "She's gone." Mo gave her hand a pat. "At least I know who... I can find out who she was."

"Maybe there's family?"

"Why were we called to clear the house, then?" Mo looked down. "And if there is anyone," Mari went on, "they won't be able to help. She won't have told anyone, see? And they'd never believe me!" Mari squeezed Mo's arm again and her friend took her hand so that the box fell between them onto the floor. Nanw looked at the papers scattered all over the place. "I nearly got there, Mo... She was still alive! She's only just gone. And she lived so close... all these years."

"Oh, don't! Don't think like that."

"So close!" Mari swallowed hard, her cheeks wet. "I... I think I need to get some air."

"I'll come with you."

Mari got up and went over to the door, a faraway look in her eyes. "No, no... I'd rather be on my –"

"But Mari! You've had a sh–" Mo started to get up.

"I'll be all right."

Mari studied Mo for a moment then smiled at her. Nodding, Mo let her go. She found a hanky somewhere, wiped her face and remained on the bed, twisting the tissue in her fist.

Mari went straight across the road without a glance at the seagulls splashing white against the sky's blue ground. The air was so cool: pure medicine if you took in deep enough gulps. She marched down the path, looking straight ahead and losing her balance now and then on the scree. Like a woman's sickening perfume, the almond scent of gorse was a wall which she passed through. She went down onto the beach and made her way towards the sea. She looked along the shore and stood stock still.

The sands were carpeted in thousands of starfish washed up in the storm. Mari walked over their bodies, releasing the foul stink of decay. The odd one was still alive and flailed a limb as she crunched it into grit. The beach was a massacre of prom frock in orange, blue and purple: the waves reeled out yet more reams of the stuff while the lively pattern struggled to slide off back to where it came from. Birds of prey were strung strategically up above, waiting for Mari to clear off. At the far end, she let her hands take the weight of her head, weeping until it ached. She sank onto her knees in the sand, realising this was the closest she had ever been to the waves. An old flame deep inside her had snuffed out. By the time she looked up, her tears had smeared the horizon to a fuzz and the beach was a feast of fallen stars for the birds to scavenge.

Chapter 28

Mari had spent the whole evening pacing up and down the bedroom like a woman in labour. Just a glimpse of that black box made her anxiously put her hand to her mouth. It was open on the bed alongside her own pile of newspaper clippings. Nanw had got much worse: it was as though some cord, wrapping itself around her body, had coiled her up tight into the foetal position so that her joints squealed for release. Mari could no longer stand it; the monkey's screaming and that flimsy flesh in spasm was making her sweat. It had been too late to fetch the vet. Nanw was weightless – a feather – and her fingers, tucked up against her face, had curled into little fists. Events had unfolded too fast for Mari to cope.

Outside, the full moon had powdered silver light along the coast, making the sea shimmer. The spiteful eyes of stars were smarting with false tears. The night was still with a sort of holy peace, the only sound, that leaking from within the house: soft footfall and the murmur of suffering. Then came the rising yowl of Nanw. It was like the wailing of a baby.

"Shshshsh," Mari pleaded, clutching her head. She couldn't pray, the noise was so intrusive. "Be quiet, now."

Mari's hands were kneading each other now and her stomach had knotted itself into a tight ball of nerves. With another contraction, Nanw's face contorted, grotesque with pain. She snarled at Mari.

"Shshshsh... please... shshshshshshshshsh." Mari sat beside her, one tear coursing down like a drop of blood. "Please don't... please be quiet... be quiet." Nanw's guts let out an unearthly growl. "Shshshsh... please be quiet. Mam can't stand it any longer!" She looked at the clock: it was getting late. The little body shook, and drivel drooled from the monkey's mouth. Nanw's eyes were closed against the horrors of the world. "Please." More fretful wails. Mari got up then changed her mind, turning around and sitting back down as though her compass were awry. Another screech and clawing of the cage bars. "Don't... Don't, sweetie pie... don't cry!" Both of them stared at each other, at their wits' end. "Please don't fight. We've had our time together."

There was a drop of blood under the monkey's nose. Nanw opened her mouth and closed it as though she were a fish out of water. Mari got up. "Shshsh... little lovely, be quiet now."

Nanw's eyes rolled in her head; howling, her whole frame ajudder. The noise echoed around the rooms, bouncing back and bruising Mari. She was on the point of collapse. The moon beamed silver softly along Nanw's dark pelt. "Please leave her be... Don't let her suffer any more," Mari prayed. Nanw grew a little quieter but then let out the screech that made Mari decide.

Mari looked out over the bay, then back at Nanw. She moved over to the cage, paused and rushed to unlock the little prison. She grasped hold of the monkey, recoiling from bony ribs and soft muscle pouches once so firm and powerful. She lifted her clear of the cage and carried her into the corridor as the wailing recommenced. She snatched one of the heavy lace frocks from its hanger and wrapped the monkey up tight.

"Stay calm, now... You'll be all right... Shshshshshshsh."

Mari pulled a shawl around her own face, tucking the ends into her collar. Holding Nanw close, she opened the door. Glancing left and right, she pulled the door shut behind her. The moon had spotlit the stile across the road: she made straight for it. She pushed past the hedgerows lining the path

122

and rushed along it, the animal bundled against her breast. She wanted no one to see her secret. She ran full-pelt where it was safe underfoot, the moans of the monkey rising into the night air.

As she whisked past, the shadow of trees made prison bars across the path. Birds were startled out of branches by the dark flying figure. In places she couldn't see her way for trees. The bundle of bones contracted and relaxed. Each step dislodged a voice inside her, one which had burrowed deeper with every passing year. The vicar's quiet voice. Blood will out. The acorn never falls far from the tree. Hackney mistress, hackney maid. His words began to leach like toxin, forming a cloud the shape of his face in her bloodstream.

She strode across the beach and stood for the short period that Nanw kept quiet. The tide was clear of starfish, the sands smooth in the silver light. The sea was still as a dead child's eye.

Mari screwed up her courage and faced the sea head on. Nanw had started up again. Mari stepped nearer to the water as the hood fell from her shoulders. Her face was white and her cheekbones hollow. The sand was soft; her deep footprint a telltale sign of her business here. The waves made a soft chant in counterpoint to the quiet weeping. Another step towards the radiant hostess of her night-time terrors, the sea. The moon too had laid down the silver carpet in welcome. The water smelled clean; Nanw's face was the picture of innocence. Mari dipped a toe into the water and its cold spread throughout her body. She inched further in, alert to any sound, and eyes fixed ahead. The stars were little flints of disinterest. She was in it up to her knees, holding the hard ball of straining gristle.

"Come on, now. You'll be OK. Come on." Her breath unfurled in the sharp air. Who, here, was she actually comforting? "Come on," two steps further in, "sweetie pie."

She was loath to trust water, that most arbitrary element. Her toes felt their way around sharp stones and sudden dips. The monkey was yowling even louder as though feeding off her fear. "It's all right..." Mari's clothes were drinking in the water; she was being sucked in up to her middle by the swell. She looked towards the horizon as though help might be found out there. The only response to come back along the shore was the echo of Nanw's anguish. Wrapped in the christening gown, the little face peeping from lace had an expression of absolute faith. "Come on..." Mari's voice was breaking up but she gripped the monkey close. The woman felt utterly lost. "Stay here. You'll be all right." Suffering had aged Nanw's face. "There was no point baptising me, see." The monkey shivered. "Water's too clean for the likes of me." Nanw looked at Mari and turned her head to listen. "Something dirty like me..." Mari scooped her hands under the monkey's arms and squeezed tightly, sensing the push and pull of the water. "Come on then." Mari's cheeks were stained with salt, "Good girl."

Pulling her close with a kiss to the forehead, Mari slid the monkey down her own body and pushed her right under, gripping the hairy shoulders tight. Nanw fought back, whipping up the water around them into white surf. Mari sobbed and the beach boomed back in longing. The monkey was fighting for its life, scratching Mari's arms until blood flowered pale in the dark blue brine. The waves broke in long, languid lines across the bay. Mari held Nanw's head under until the water around them was still. The lace limply swished its surrender to the icy waves. Though now unseeing, Nanw's marble eyes were witness to what had happened, and they were still staring up at her through the clear water. She let the small hands go; let the sea take the monkey slowly out into the black blankness.

Mari hadn't realised that her arms were bleeding. The sea was completely calm now, and it was so cold. Mari kept listening out but there was only silence. For the time being, the echo was keeping mum.

Chapter 29

Mari had been sleeping for days since she'd come back soaking wet from the beach and gone to bed fully dressed. Her clothes had dried stiffly on her and the salt water had helped heal the scratches on her arms. Eventually she got up, washed and put on clean clothes. She ate some food from the basket Mo had left her on the step. When she caught sight of Nanw's empty nest by the window, she felt a twinge. Poor sweet Nanw, may she rest in peace. Still though, she seemed to have gained a new lease of life: she was calm and her burden was gone. Although she hadn't yet been out, she was free now to come and go as she pleased.

Mari was in no rush to return to her mother's house. Her search was over: whatever it was she was meant to know would come to her in due course. She had felt at home there, at least. And her mother had kept the stories of her baby's discovery. So surely she had feelings towards her? It was enough to keep Mari going for the time being.

She hadn't been able to face cleaning up after Nanw immediately. She'd left the cage and its mess just as it was until today, when the stench had driven her to take action. Mari washed all the blankets, she dried and ironed them before putting them away in a bin bag beside the box under her bed. She swilled out the food bowls and scooped up the damp newspaper from the base of the cage. Nanw had been a lively presence in the house, pulling Mari's hair, stealing her bracelet or scratching spitefully every time she was disturbed. Only now she was alone could Mari make a clean breast of things.

She peeled off the cardboard underneath and caught sight of what was – after a fashion – a stash stowed away in a corner of the cage. A pound coin, some nuts and one of Mari's bracelets. She smiled sadly. So Nanw'd had a few escapades then, had she? Mari put the treasures up on the mantelpiece. She cleaned the cage and let the air circulate while she brushed up all the muck around it with a yard brush.

On her way to the best room, she opened the front door and took in a deep gulp of fresh air. Summer, about to lessen its grip, had warmed the hedgerows, swelling the nuts into rosy cheeks of nobodies. She let herself down gradually and knelt by Nanw's toy box. Softly, softly... lift up the lid... Beady eyes cross-questioned her. She took the toys out one by one and put them into a fresh plastic sack. The teddy she had bought in the market; a chiming ball that timed each playsession; a piece of colourful rope for teething. Mari pushed them all right out of sight. Like a Chinese box with a secret at its heart, the chest was empty now except for the leather jewellery casket and inside that, the emerald in its white rag. Mari closed the jewels away and, sighing, tied a knot in the sack.

Hearing someone clearing their throat, she got up awkwardly.

"Gwyn!"

"I'm sorry... but... but the door was open."

"Don't worry!"

Mari glanced down at the sack hiding by her feet. Gwyn noticed she was lacklustre and had lost more than a little weight.

"Oh... I've brought," he paused, "brought the clock for you to have a look at." He had a jewellery box tucked between thumb and forefinger.

"Oh."

"If it's a bad time..."

"No... no, it's fine," Mari replied. Gwyn smiled. "This way." He followed Mari into the bedroom, sitting by the empty cage without comment. "I'll go and make us some tea."

Mari went into the kitchen, glad to have the chance to think. She found a spare mug and wetted the teabags, carrying the drinks back carefully. He was standing with his back to her, studying the stuff on the mantelpiece. Gwyn turned and took his tea gratefully.

"You're from a big family..." Mari looked down at her mug.

"Big family..." He picked up the picture of the bicycling girl. "Your mother?"

Mari looked up sharply. "What?"

"She's just like you... like your mother would look..."

What to say? She glanced at the open door of the cage. "No," she said eventually. "Mam's just died."

Gwyn's smile disappeared. "Oh, sorry to hear that..." At last she could mention her mother without misrepresenting her. He raised an eyebrow. "Were you close?"

Mari gave a crooked smile. "I wouldn't say that, no." She went to sit on the bed.

"It's always a shock, though, isn't it?" Mari agreed. "But she's gone to a better place..." Gwyn went past her to sit down on the bed beside her.

"D'you think so?"

"Well..."

"To heaven?" Mari asked, her heart racing.

"That's what I tell myself..." He paused and his eyes clouded over slightly. "Mari..." He was gripping his mug tighter and you could see pain etched around his eyes. "My wife..."

"I know," Mari said and he relaxed. She wouldn't make him say those words. Gwyn looked up in tears. Mari swallowed hard. "I'm sorry."

"I do like to think there's a heaven," he said, his eyes wide. Mari smiled. "Of course."

Silence was a soft old blanket enfolding the pair while the steam from their tea rose like incense.

"Did you know that babies," Gwyn started musing, "babies dream in the womb, you know?" Mari was taken aback. "When we were trying for a baby, I was reading about it... They dream, you know? But what do they dream about if there's no heaven?" This set Mari thinking. "They haven't seen anything in their lives but still they dream about something, in the dark." Mari thought about the mute faces she'd just stuffed into a bin bag. They looked at each other almost tenderly. "I'm sorry I didn't say anything..."

"No need," Mari replied.

"I hadn't told anybody."

"Of course not." A breeze had drawn through the house, setting the cage door swinging. "Shall we have a look at that clock, then?"

Gwyn came back to earth and started opening his box. Their shared secrets were out of the bottle and snaking out of the door on a sweet draught of air.

"I've done the case and set all the gems... They're, well, fabulous." The ague in his hands made progress slow. "It's just like I'd imagined." He took out the diminutive timepiece wrapped in tissue. His fingers teased it apart as though it were his own birthday present. He put it on his palm and grinned at Mari. "What d'you think?" The watch had been transformed into a fine grandfather clock, one gemstone at each hour. "I've been reading up on it," he went on, smiling. "At midnight – and midday! – we've got jet, for mourning... Then there's amethyst to stop you taking to drink..." Mari smiled back. "Turquoise to protect –" Gwyn scratched his head.

"Sailors," Mari came to his rescue.

"Yes!" The clock was a masterpiece. "I haven't wound it up yet. Thought you might like to..."

"Me?"

"Why not?"

"Oh, no... I'm not..."

"Come on. Open just here and wind it up." Behind a door in its belly was a weeny handle. Mari took the clock and felt her fingers fumble over the finely tuned workings.

"Turn it tight enough to set the spring. Then it can go into the house. Nearly finished it now!"

Listening to it notch up moments click by click, she wound the knob until it would go no further. Set up on the slate mantel, it beamed mildly like a mini moon willing to forgive all misdemeanours. Small as it was, it gave her hearth a new focus, one where the present and future counted more than commonplaces such as scale. Mari closed the slot on the back of the clock. The pair sat magnetised by its little face, its figures glowing with possibility. Trembling for a few unmarked seconds between time zones, the arms jerked suddenly forward.

Chapter 30

The main market windows had been boarded up, making it dark and cool. The building work wouldn't start for months but already surveyors were striding about, taking over the place with their measurements and photographs. Mo cocked an eyebrow then stuck out her tongue behind one man's back to make Mari laugh.

The two of them were packing up Mo's stall. She'd been running her stock down lately and discounting heavily: Everything Must Go! Some elderly women had already helped her clear the decks by buying up bargains in the way of aprons and housecoats. The feather boa from her display tossed about her neck and cigarette in mouth, Mo was busy taping up a box.

"Depressing, isn't it!" She took out the cigarette to talk. "But at least we've had our innings, eh? Remember when that man bought some knickers off me and his wife brought them back next day asking who he was getting them for!" They both grinned. "And that other bloke wanting bloomers for himself!" With her belly bobbing and tears spurting everywhere, Mo looked like fizzy pop about to explode. Mari carried on smiling at her. "Takes all sorts, I'm telling you. But all good things come to an end."

The women spent a few hours putting the towels, knickers and dishcloths away. Mo folded a nest of petticoats and underwear for Mari into a carrier bag. Mo was looking sadly at the empty stall so Mari went to buy them both a cup of tea as the kettle had been packed. They sat amid the stack of boxes, talking to other stallholders who were calling by with good-luck cards. The caretaker had bought them a bouquet and Mo made them all laugh by insisting he give her a noisy kiss. Iwan came over to bid them farewell with a miniature rose bush each for the women and a bottle of whisky for Dai. He asked them to plant out the roses to remind them of him. It was quiet when everyone had gone away.

"I'm going back there tonight if you want to come," Mo murmured.

Mari glanced at her and thought of the old house overlooking the sea.

"N... not sure."

"Might help?" Mo suggested.

Gwyn's clock ticked in the back of her mind.

"OK, then, maybe I will come," Mari agreed after a long pause.

Mo got up and spat onto her sleeve, using it to polish up the old copper rule on the counter.

"Well," Mo said, tilting their polystyrene cups together in a muted toast, "here's to a new start!"

Mari smiled at her. "Good luck, Mo."

"We could both do with a bit of that."

Mari could not get out of the habit of chaperoning her jewellery box, and took it with her on their way to her mother's. Mo had been chatting about the new business, how she and Dai would have to step things up a gear if they were to recover lost income from the stall. The women got out and watched sunset seeping across the walls. The days were drawing in and the brambles in the garden were loaded with blackberries spoilt by rain. Mari tipped up her chin and went up the path. Had she been there as a little girl? Surely her mother had been worried about her: why keep the clippings otherwise? Well, it was better than nothing. But quite a risk, when you thought about it: anyone could have found the box and started asking awkward questions. Maybe she took them out every now and then for a little look, too. She'd entrusted her baby to a vicar: that meant she might be religious.

"Ready?" Mo put the key in the lock. Mari nodded. The kitchen was as they had left it on the night of the storm. Mari led the way while Mo paused beside the table to ask, "Do... do you want to pray?"

This was the first time that Mo had ever volunteered to pray.

"No... not tonight."

Mo raised an eyebrow.

"I've done my fair share of praying," Mari said and the subject was closed.

The house had retained its warmth. Mo went off to tip out the kitchen drawers into black bin bags.

Mari couldn't remember whether there had been any photographs in the living room. There was nothing above the fireplace except a few gardening magazines, a telescope to capture the view and a pair of spectacles. Mari picked them up. Perhaps her mother got headaches too? She was lucky at least that *she* didn't need glasses. Nothing much else of interest, really. A door opened onto a broad flight of stairs with a stained-glass window half way up. Mari pulled herself slowly up each step, taking it all at her own pace. Her mother would have been the last person to touch the banister. On the wide and airy landing stood a bookshelf lined with beautiful books. Mari liked reading, too. Four doors off the landing: three bedrooms and a bathroom, by the looks of it.

The master bedroom was neat, with a big wooden bed facing the sea view. Mari ran her finger over the wood at the bed's base. Wasn't broken, nothing underneath. She took a peek under the blanket and touched the dent her mother's body had made in the mattress. On the dressing table were scent, and a brush which Mari picked up, realising it was hairless. She traced her fingers over the bottle's womanly curves and plucked out the glass stopper. She breathed in the perfume deeply. Expensive make-up. Clearly kept herself looking good; perhaps she'd been a beauty in the flesh as well as in Mari's dreams.

Mari opened one or two drawers: tights, socks, knickers. She pulled out another drawer and smelt the clothing inside, steeped in someone's scent. She buried her face in it. Jumpers, blouses: all good quality. A lady with taste. Mari slotted the drawer back. No letters here. No bedside table either, nor a diary left on a chair as a casual clue to a character's identity. Mari drank in the view her mother had enjoyed before getting up each morning. Three fingerprints smeared the window's handle: she placed her own fingers on them, one on each. She could hear Mo moving around downstairs.

On the windowsill of the guest room were flesh flowers that had withered. A stylish chest and wardrobe had already been emptied. And now for the last one; must be the box room. She froze. A doll was on the bed, sitting plumply on the pillow like a baby, dark eyes unblinking. Mari went over to the bed and snatched it up. There were no other signs of children in the house. Just this one doll which Mari clutched close to her chest.

"Mari. Mari!"

Mari peered down the stairwell, keeping a firm hold on canvas limbs.

"What?"

"Mari! Come quick!" Mo implored.

Mari's heart quickened. Pressing "Baby" to her breast, she rushed downstairs and was out of breath by the time she

136

reached the kitchen. There was a man standing on the threshold.

Mari looked confused.

"This... gentleman... neighbour... is asking whether I'd mind going to see the lady who used to live here. In the home... Wants us to give her a card."

Mari pressed Baby tight. Mo looked at her, wide-eyed.

"Mari, she's still alive!"

Chapter 31

The home, with its white walls, was clean and clinical. Windows looking out over the surrounding gardens were intended to make residents feel a part of the world. Mo was parked near the entrance, smoking nervously. Trying to make the best impression, Mari had changed her outfit half a dozen times before plumping for a long-sleeved blouse which covered the scars from Nanw's scratches. As she'd tidied her hairdo with a wet comb and a little hairspray, she wondered how much her mother would look like her. Should she buy flowers? No, better not. Worrying, she had got ready far too early and was waiting outside ready with her bag when Mo had come to fetch her. Mari went up to reception. A young nurse was behind the desk.

Mari opened her mouth and the nurse smiled encouragingly.

"I'm... I'm here to see..." She stumbled over the name.

"Who?"

" Mrs... Eunice... James."

"Eunice?"

"Yes." Mari twisted her fingers into a knot. The nurse seemed perplexed but then grinned.

"That's nice! Hardly gets any visitors, she does, apart from a neighbour now and then. Sign here, please." Picking up the biro, Mari tried to steady her nerves. "Friends, are you?" The nurse's teeth were white.

"Mm."

"Great! She's in the day room. Know your way around?"

"No."

"I'll take you down there then," the nurse glanced in the visitors' book, "Mari."

Mari's footsteps lagged behind the nurse's. "Between you and me... just so you know what to expect, she's not been herself lately, well, a few years since, to be honest." Oh, heavens. "Poor thing! Calling for her daughter all the time. We've asked around, but she hasn't got any children. She won't believe us, though, however many times we tell her!" Dear God. "Mari? Didn't mean to scare you. Just – forearmed is forewarned – or whatever. When d'you last see Eunice?" When, indeed... "Are you all right? Glass of water?"

Someone came out of the room they were heading for, giving Mari a glimpse of a woman in a wheelchair facing the window.

"I don't think I can..." Mari wasn't ready for this, after all. "It's not right."

She had imagined this reunion every day since she was a little girl: it had always made up a big part of her prayers. In her childhood, of course, she'd made her mother beautiful, clever and full of fun. As a young woman, she'd made her honest and kind. She'd had her mother take a new role every time Mari's own life had changed.

"Mari?" The nurse was holding the door open. "Come in. Eunice is over here."

Mari took a few steps into the room. It was large and airy: against the picture windows wrapping around its walls were pressed the perfect cheeks of late summer roses. Someone coughed. The TV was murmuring somewhere. The nurse indicated the woman in the wheelchair. "You've half an hour until dinnertime." The silvery hair was thinning, her shoulders upturned nests perched either side of her ears. She was trembling. As though she were amid circles set off by a

140

pebble thrown from a lake's far shore. An elderly man staggered past them both. Mari approached her from behind. What could she say? The old lady had already seen her ghost reflected in the window.

"Who are you?" Eunice didn't look round. Mari froze then moved in a little semicircle to stand before her. They looked at each other. "You're old," she told Mari. Sweet Lord, help! Her mother's face was exactly the same shape as her own. Her watery eyes were hard to read. She was as light as a bird and wrapped tight in a white blanket. "Sit down." Eunice pointed with a shaky finger at a nearby chair. "Come closer, so I can see you properly. It's nice having a visitor." Her skin was dry and her voice a whisper. Mari drew her chair up. They had the same hands, too. "How do I know you, then?"

Mari's heart sank. "A friend," she suggested quietly.

"Dinnertime soon!"

"Yes."

The old lady's head was nodding. She kept looking out of the window as though in search of something. "Look at those roses."

"Aren't they pretty," Mari agreed.

"Yes they are."

"Do you like gardening?" No harm in asking.

"Don't know; do I?"

"Well, yes you do. You've got a big garden back home."

Eunice's eyes flicked along Mari's face as though there were answers in it.

"I grew up on a farm," she said.

"Did you?"

"Yes. Liked flowers... that sort of thing... liked running in the boggy fields. Mam'd go mad when I came back with my clothes a mess. Springtime, there'd be lady's smock all down my frock – aren't they the flowers cuckoos spit on? Summer

I'd have cottongrass in my hair like dandruff! And Mam would give us buttermilk to drink…" Happy tales of mare and foal always made Mari jealous. "Look like someone?" Eunice studied Mari carefully. Her daughter nodded. "You look familiar." The shakes had taken hold of the old woman's body. Eunice looked down at her own hands. "Can't stop trembling. I'm like this all day long."

"I'm sorry."

"Too bad: that's the way the world is. Can't even hold a book any more. Used to love reading, as well." Mari's face relaxed. The woman leaned forward so that they were almost nose to nose. She'd never been this close to anyone. "Between you and me, mind… electric shock therapy makes you forget a lot." She settled back in her chair and laughed. They both watched the flowers outside. "My daughter likes her books, too." Mari looked up at her. "She's very busy; teacher, she is." Mari put her hand on the arm of Eunice's chair. "Much too busy to come and see me! Two children and her husband working at the bank. Lives in town, lovely house. Want for nothing, they do!" Mari tasted the tang of lies on the air. "I'm tired now." Mari drew her hand back. "Nearly dinnertime."

"Yes it is," answered Mari.

"Off you go, then," Eunice gave Mari a brisk nod.

"Oh, OK then." Mari got up shakily then paused. Eunice was trembling even more than before. Mari turned to go but the mother took her daughter's hand.

"When you come next time, bring some buttermilk, will you?"

Those familiar eyes were beautiful. "Of course I will."

Her mother let go of her hand. Eunice looked past Mari's shoulder at the light with its big globe lampshade.

"'*Moonlight becomes you*,'" she crooned.

"Ah," Mari laughed.

Mari moved away and Eunice turned back to the roses shedding their petals onto the lawn.

In the corridor, she could hear the clatter of plates from the kitchen.

"Everything OK?" asked the nurse at the desk.

Mari's tears had long ago been spent and she managed to wave at the nurse and let the wide doors swing shut behind her.

"See you again," the nurse called, going back to her paperwork.

Mari went over to the car parked in the grounds. Mo turned on the ignition and said nothing, knowing her friend needed time to recover. Mari swivelled round to look back at the big window. Writ small against the glass the figure of her mother looked off into the distance beyond what was left of the season's last roses.

Chapter 32

It wasn't easy to dismantle the cage. The screws had rusted and were stiff. Each bar of the door had to be removed one by one. The radio had been moved onto the mantelpiece; having the news of an evening brought Mari back into the world again. The emerald was being set into a ring by a jeweller's in town. Mari couldn't wait to get it back.

Her visit to her mother had been preying on her mind so long she felt ill. It was too late, wasn't it? She could hardly blame her mother for losing her marbles. All the same, surely she'd go mad unless she kept her hands busy. She turned a screw in the latch to loosen it but ended up having to tug at the door.

Car headlights spilled along the road, blinking off outside the house. Dafydd, in a blind panic, leaping out. He snapped the passenger door open, causing Sara to fall head first into his arms. Mari ran over to the door.

Dafydd came up the path carrying his mother. He pushed past Mari into the bedroom and laid his mother down gently on the bed.

"I can't wake her." Dafydd shifted his weight from one leg to the other, his hands together in a half-prayer for salvation. "I didn't know what else to do." The body was limp. Sara's face was white and her lips dark blue. The body of Dafydd's father had looked like that when she'd arrived at the scene of the car-crash. Dafydd had been there too, and his expression had been just as helpless then as it was now. "Mana!" Dafydd gasped. "Please!"

Mari went up to the body, which stank of beer. She couldn't have eaten for days. Mari leant over and listened to her shallow breathing. Sara's eyes were rolling back in her head.

"Sara... Can you hear me?" Mari shook her by the shoulders.

"Don't know what to do," Dafydd repeated, backing towards the window. "Maybe she's taken something."

"Sara!" Mari slapped her cheek. "Sara!" A rumble came from within. "We need to get the poison out... How long's she been like this?" Dafydd stood there like a shop mannequin. Mari rolled the floppy body over to the side of the bed, turning her onto her side. Sara's skin was sweaty. She gave Dafydd an impatient glance. "Go get a bucket, man! Quick!"

Once he'd returned, Mari opened Sara's mouth with one hand and pushed her fingers down her throat, pressing on the fleshy parts. Before long Sara grabbed her belly and dark muck spurted into the bucket. She gagged and gave a cough. There were no solids in the liquid streaming from her mouth.

Dafydd shuffled up to his mother. "Mam?" Sara's eyes blinked to clear the fuzzy picture of her son. "Mam?" She was sick again. Mari rubbed her back. "Mam!"

"Fetch hot water, a flannel and a cold drink," Mari commanded.

Sara was breathing heavily. Mari washed her face, trying not to think whose mouth she was dabbing, whose brow was being wiped. Dafydd watched them both. She put the water to her lips, supporting her head as though she were a baby. Then she took the bucket out the back to pour the bile down the drain. Mari returned to find Dafydd sitting by the bed. Sara was twirling tendrils of his hair close to his ear. Mari stood in the shadows by the door. So they *did* share some bond, then. Sara noticed her and Dafydd got up.

"You can go now," she told him.

"But…"

"She needs a rest."

Dafydd nodded and his mother smiled at him.

"I'll be back…"

"She'll be fine by morning."

Mari followed him and before he slipped out into the night, Dafydd gave her a grateful glance.

Back in the bedroom, she watched Sara trying to sleep on the narrow bed. Through heavy lids she looked at Mari and said, "Thanks."

Mari avoided looking at her by picking up a towel and hanging it by the fire to dry. She picked up the cup for Sara then went to fetch some bread and butter from the kitchen. She fed her morsel by morsel. "This'll mop up any toxins you've got left in you," Mari told her. The skin on Sara's face was taut. "That boy's seen far more than he should, you know."

"You loved him, didn't you?" Sara asked, relaxing back onto the bed.

"Doesn't matter now." Mari went over to sit by the empty cage. The colour was starting to come back into Sara's cheeks.

"It *does* matter, though," Sara persisted. Mari paused. "You'd have loved him better than I did," Sara confessed, the rings around her eyes darkening to purple.

"I didn't love him in the way you mean, not in the way you loved him… I didn't want to take him away from you…" Sara made no reply. "Think what you like," Mari shrugged. "I loved him only as a brother. We were kindred spirits… knew what each other was thinking, had the same interests." Tears were running out of Sara's eyes in a straight line down her pillow. "I've never loved anyone except as a brother. Maybe there's something wrong with me." There, Mari had said it. "Have you... have you ever felt utterly lost... then found yourself only because someone offered you a shoulder to lean on?" Sara opened her eyes. Her husband had always lent her his shoulder, too. Mari's eyes were dreamy and she looked quite old. This was the first time Sara had seen her properly. Her forehead was like a schoolbook: narrow feint-ruled. Her dark eyes were rather deep-set. Sara felt fatigue sweep her body. "I couldn't believe it the first time I saw him," Mari continued. "We looked like peas in a pod: could have been related!" Mari's chin dipped onto her chest. "I'm sorry," she told Sara and started to weep. Sara's hair hung in damp curtains either side of her face. She reached out her hand to comfort Mari. "When I found them in the car after the accident... they were both still alive. I went to his dad first but his legs were stuck... Then it was too late..." Mari stroked Sara's thumb. "I wasn't strong enough to get him out and anyway he was gone within minutes... I only just managed to get Dafydd out." The film played on, no less painful for being familiar. Was Sara sleeping? Mari closed her eyes. That man could easily have been her brother. "He asked me to look after you!" Mari blurted and her cheeks flushed in shame.

Mari pushed her head onto Sara's pillow, her tears adding to the dark patch of linen by Sara's ear. Playing over in the heads of both women was the reel of that terrible night. Sara raised a hand and touched Mari's head lightly. Mari recalled all those times her father had blessed every other child in the church: all save her. All she needed right now was Sara's tender touch: her blessing told Mari she was forgiven.

Chapter 33

They shared a breakfast together, a boiled egg each, and then Sara went home. With a blanket thrown over her, Mari had fallen asleep in the chair. She had actually enjoyed Sara's company, and had even lent her a clean jumper to take home. Time was too short to carry on dismantling the cage: she would take the whole thing out into the front garden. Wearing old clothes and workboots, she started to drag it across the lino, bringing a wave of trapped air with it which only broke at the threshold when the contraption was hurled topsy-turvy onto the lawn. She had been fortified by a few full nights of sleep.

Autumn mist was winding through the hedgerows. The desiccating leaves seemed slippery. Boxes of rubbish still lined the corridor: Mari grabbed them and took them out there, too. The pile by the cage grew bigger as Mari got into her stride. From the best room she took the boxes of papers she'd purloined from other people's lives. The old bag of Nanw's toys she'd felt so guilty about was swung from the doorway onto the heap. She was as high as a kite. She swept the photos from the mantelpiece in her room, frames and all, into a bin bag. Nanw's bedding went out too. Every letter, every picture, full drawers, whole boxes, went into the sack. Not even the correspondence of the quiet man escaped this fate. The only records that deserved respect were her own: the pair of boxes from under the bed, which she placed facing each other on the pillow. Out in the breeze, the papers flapped like startled seagulls but Mari pinned them down.

Back in the best room she pursued memories with an imaginary broom. Pictures came off the wall and boxes of books were upended. She opened Nanw's toy box and took out the white rag that had been home to the emerald. It had been snug in it all these years, like Baby Bunting in his rabbit skin. The gown hadn't been warm enough, though, to stop a baby crying on a chilly dawn church doorstep. It was the one she'd worn when they'd made her a foundling. Now it was grey and falling apart in her fingers. She crumpled it into her fist and, taking it outside, she made of it a crown atop the heap.

Mari scoured out the guts of the cottage, leaving them trailing their drool on the green bed of grass. The debris of her whole life towered over her. Friendly faces. Love letters not to herself, but missives nevertheless. Souls gone missing who had stayed in her company awhile. She went back into the house and fetched the big Bible borrowed from someone else's family. She knew it chapter and verse so she wouldn't really miss it. Lugging it over to the bonfire, matches in pocket, she stuffed it into a niche, a paperweight which would trample all those wasteful words.

She scraped the match with ceremony. It needed a cupping hand against the wind to encourage the flame but soon it was licking the papers like a faithful dog. The words, panicking, ran into each other like ink then entered the ether. The heat blistered the photographs, making ugly the faces of her old beloveds. Wind and fire had linked arms; were whirling together like death-defying dervishes.

Mari remembered the boxes still on her pillow, twin caches kept close all this time by their keepers. She could lift each with one finger. Taking out the sets of matching photos, she studied each pair then set the duplicate babies up on the mantel. The empty boxes were slung onto the fire, disturbing a few papers: again they took the garb of seagulls to make their getaway. For a moment, they were white against the grey smoke but their singed wings soon fell, failing, back into the flames.

The glass in the photo frames started to crack, shamelessly letting the heat in to deface her former family members. This was almost fun! Her spirits were rising with the filthy flumes flying off into the trees. Her face was bright red and her eyes were watering but it was the fire's fault, not hers. The memories were leaving in a sooty plume of smoke. They left an acrid taste in Mari's throat. She coughed then put her arm across her mouth so that she could breathe through the filter of her sleeve.

The books took an age to burn, their pages glued together by gravitas. Mari used a branch to prop them open so that oxygen could conspire with fire to consume them. Every chapter must be burnt. Everything must go. She became systematic, and the poker was her bayonet in the battle against those books and photos, letters and lies. The Bible got it in the spine and bled its river of gilt. The cover was dislodged and its cross shrivelled to the size of a toenail. A page proclaiming, "Be baptised", went up in smoke.

She kept a hold on her army until all was ash. The walls were hidden by a dirty pillar of soot which had left its twin smeared along the whitewash. The cage had split open, its black bars lying in soft light powder like men fallen in some desert campaign and charred to bone. So who would tell their loves back home? Mari paused, her clothes and hair stinking of bonfire.

She stepped round half of the fire's circle and went into the empty house. Filling a basin with water, she plopped some flannels into it and took off all her things. She stood in the kitchen to wash every part of her body, scrubbing away at the lipstick kisses of smoke. She pressed a cloth against her nape and forehead, poking its corner into her eyes to clear out sleep and smut. Using her hands as a cup, she rinsed herself all over, letting water stream down her legs and across the floor. Bare as a baby, she stood shivering in a shallow pool. When she washed her hair over the sink, some droplets sprinkled her forehead. Be baptised, she told herself. That particular dream swirled out of the window to join the rest.

Still naked, Mari drank glass after glass of cold water to dilute the taste in her mouth. She took in so much liquid, her belly felt tight. Outside, the smoke had died right down. She rubbed herself dry with a rough towel. She put on clean clothes, leaving the dirty ones in a pile by the sink. She boiled the kettle and, for once, she took her tea with two sugars.

Now that the cage had gone from the bedroom, she could sit properly in the window to admire the world at her leisure. The identical babies above the hearth were still there side by side, and were company enough for her, too. And although all that passed for a view tonight was a dark scorchmark in the middle of the lawn, her senses were more alert than usual. Mari could feel the cold of an evening close to the year's tail-end. The plethora of possessions in each room had muffled each separate sound into hubbub. Now each thought rapped against the empty wall and came pealing back like an old, old song she'd heard anew. She could even hear starlings roost. A different bird came to mind, though, one far from his nest: that cormorant she'd seen on lookout over the ocean.

Chapter 34

Gwyn had been winnowing the tideline for hours, although his sack was empty, slumped like a sulky spouse beside him on the sand. Even though the waves were hardly stirring, he was determined he'd find wheat among the chaff. He'd become so desperate he was on all fours like a cuckold going through his wife's things for evidence.

For the first time ever, Mari paddled along the shallows. It hadn't felt right to pray since she had drowned Nanw. Unable to stand the cold and her own company at home, she was spending most of her days wandering outside. The green ring was a regular feature on her finger. She would steal glances at it as if it meant the very renewal of her marriage vows. Gwyn didn't notice her at first, blinkered as he was to all but his square patch of petty territory.

He looked up at her suddenly. In shirtsleeves, the soft white of his arm was showing, studded with black gravel. Mari had until now never seen him look anything other than collected. She smiled at him. Realising the knees of his cords were wet, he got up.

"Any luck?"

"No... there's nothing here. Been up and down, up and down... seen nothing!" His eyes were swivelling. "Usually I get *something*..."

His fingers were fretted with cuts. "Your hands, they're..."

Gwyn glowered at her. "Nothing! There's always something... I don't believe it." He looked back along the beach.

Mari looked out to sea. "It looks so flat today," Mari said. "Those waves couldn't carry a catfish!"

"But she always sends me something," he barked. Mari looked at him in surprise. "Always sends something." He blinked at her. "I'm... I'm sorry..."

"Don't worry. I'll leave you in peace!"

"Mari... please." He seemed to be some stranger who still had the power to disappoint her. Gwyn fell silent and looked down at the bag. "She always sends me something." A breeze cooled Mari's cheeks. "We... we'd come here together all the time... every day, nearly." His vista was a world that had gone. "She loved it... and when she was ill, she said... she said she'd always be right here." The wind cut between them for an instant. "And when I came down here that first morning... there was something for me on the beach... a little broken cup." Mari wondered what he meant. "It was after she'd –" He couldn't say it. "That night before, I'd dropped a teacup." Mari took a step towards him, feeling electricity all around them. The clear sky was the flat sea in a mirror; every sound was magnified. "She always sends me messages but," he squinted left and right, "there's nothing here today." His face had darkened, making the lines around his mouth look deeper. "She's in a mood with me, I bet. Should have looked after her better, Mari." She shuffled closer to him, feeling she was letting something go. Sobbing now, his arms were hanging limp and his shoulders were hunched. Mari tried to hold him but he slipped through her grasp onto his knees. She knelt down with him in the middle of the seaweed, and he cupped her face in his hands. "And now there's no sign of her at all."

The surf slid on and off the waves with a spiteful chuckle. Gwyn gazed at Mari until she peeled away to sit down among the wet tentacles. He crumpled beside her and the pair listened to the sea grind the grit in its teeth.

Resting on Mari's lap, Gwyn wept on. She laid her hand on his head and nursed him. Unlike most, Mari was not afraid of other people crying, would never rush to fetch an adult a cup of tea or a sweet for a child to stopper their sobbing. How can you get better if you don't ever let the poison out? Gwyn, growing calmer, looked up and over to the line where sun and sky were separated. Sitting there with him in the meagre debris the sea had cast away, Mari felt like Crusoe alone on his first day.

Chapter 35

Mo and Mari unhooked the remaining clothes from the back of the stall. Dai was smoking by the entrance, waiting with the van to clear Mari's stock. Until the next auction where they could sell the best items, she would share Mo's little storage cell. There were hardly any stallholders and still fewer shoppers. The big hall was quiet for the first time in years, the life dribbled out of it like sawdust. Even Iwan had given up on the place; he had no café to hang around until its reincarnation on the new site. At the far end was Dafydd's unit, all boarded up. The smell of fresh bread, though, was the same as ever, as was the sight of the girls from the baker's on their tea break. As she helped Mari, Mo was trying to avoid even a peek at her own stall next door with its weighty padlock. Mo was glad to see Mari wearing the emerald ring.

There was quite a bit left over, most especially bags, gloves and items of gold and silver which were not worth enough to auction. Some minor dealer might take them as one lot... Mari plucked the rings from their velvet mouths and dropped them into a soft black bag where they chinked together in their new nest. Dai took out the boxes to the van and Mo brushed the floor. The cream cameos were smiling amicably from their dark cushions. Mari emptied the display case and chose a couple of glass brooches for the delighted bakery girls.

Except for a box of combs and knick-knacks which would be easy to get rid of, most of it was now gone. Apart, that is, from a string of thick, hand-blown glass globes bobbing in all colours above the stand. They were antique fishing floats

157

she'd got in the early days from a mariner, in exchange for a gold band. He'd told her how they were used in witchcraft as a crystal ball. How selling them would court bad luck but buying them, disaster. A straight swap was the only solution. But once the deal was done, they warded off evil. Mari stretched up to unhook the transparent talismans. They were so pretty when they caught the light. She cradled one of them in her palm so that the dust came off, leaving a clear eye of colour.

Dai and Mo had returned.

"These are all that's left," Mari told them.

Mari offered Mo the glass baubles. "What?" Mo smiled.

"For you!"

"Thought you had to do a swapsie? You said..." Mari gave a nod. "I'll think of something to give you," Mo added.

"Good luck, Mo."

Mo looked at Mari, puzzled. "Since when've you been superstitious?" Winking, Mo took the string of clinking magic.

Mari smiled at her friend. Leaving the key on her counter, Mari took a fond last look around while Mo and Dai removed what was left of her last things. The weak sun had transformed a glass case into a snow dome, thumbprints marking every sale she'd made, drifting down into perpetuity. Mari wasn't planning to dust them off.

As she walked towards the exit, Dafydd came into her mind, unbidden. Turning back, she decided to say goodbye properly and went over to his stall. This was where she'd first met his father, when Dafydd had just been a small boy in the middle of it all, swamped by an oversized butcher's coat. He'd been in his element. His dad laughing as he rolled up the long sleeves. The lad had grown into that coat, though. Behind this shutter, he had stood joking with his customers. She looked closer. Blood was flowing under the door! She pressed an ear against the wood. She could hear movement. Fear rolled over her in waves.

"Dafydd!" A bakery girl came over and ran to fetch help. "Dafydd, is that you?" The blood swirling outwards was scarlet. Mari felt faint. "Dafydd!" She kicked the door and tugged at the lock but she couldn't dislodge it. "Please, someone! Help!"

Dai arrived with a crowbar; on his heels Mo, who caught Mari's hand and pulled her away. He levered the lock open, the girls watching the scene with their hands over their mouths.

Dafydd was lying in the shape of a cross. His torso was bare and there were little stab wounds all over his body and a knife on the floor. The blood was spurting from his wrists. Mari knelt in the sticky pool beside him. His lips were twisted into some sort of smile. The chain, her birthday present, was at his neck. He opened his mouth, "Mmm..." The blood was taking his strength away. "M... Mana..."

Mari leant over him, their brows almost bumping. "Shshshsh... be quiet, lovely... just rest." He tried to speak again. "Shshshsh... no need to talk."

Mari did her best to stem the flow and tried to ignore the emerald ring which was flashing its go-ahead green at the failing young man.

Chapter 36

A rust-red streaking stain across her clothes, Mari sat in the overheated waiting room. The smell of blood had grown so strong that passers-by were glancing in at her. She'd had to remove Dafydd's chain as part of the admissions' procedure and worried every one of the golden links with her fingers. One of the girls had gone to fetch the young man's mother while Mari had stayed with him in the ambulance, every little wound spilling his whole life across the floor. But he was young, they said: that at least was in his favour. Mari couldn't stand that green eye so she'd taken the ring off. All those little cuts along his skin! The emerald had tricked her after all; she stuffed it way down into her pocket.

For the first time since Nanw had drowned, Mari began to pray, rubbing the thick loops as though they were rosary beads. She shut her eyes and made a simple request: the boy's life. She herself had hurt him just as much as his mother. She prayed that he would survive and lead a happy life free from shadow. Now that her former prayer had been answered – more or less – she could afford to keep this one short.

Someone rushed by, letting the door swing open. She saw Dafydd's limp body, quite still, like some saint prone atop his cist in a chilly church. The blood had stained the bedding beneath each wrecked wrist. His skin was pale and studded with sweat, his lips were purple. Staring straight ahead – his eyes marble blanks just like Nanw's under the waves – he seemed witness to Paradise or some Paradise lost.

At the market, his pulse pumping blood out pointlessly,

she had kept pressing his wrists as though she were the Dutch Boy stemming the dyke. Laid out on a stretcher, they'd wrapped him in bandages like a mummy with Mari at his side.

Mari had been sitting on a plastic bench with her eyes closed when a nurse came to sit beside her. She blinked awake, expecting the worst.

"He's not doing too badly... Stopped bleeding at last and he's had a transfusion. He's a strong man: he's lucky. You caught him just in time." Mari sobbed, hiding her face. "Oh, listen... he'll be fine. Mind you, he meant business." Mari looked at her. "In some cases, it's just a cry for help, but this one: he'd decided. He'll need someone to look after him." Tears were pearling in Mari's lower eyelids. "Try not to worry, though. You can come and see him in a bit." She patted Mari's shoulder as she got up.

He'll need someone to look after him.

The waiting-room door opened on Sara, who stared at the state of Mari's clothes. She ran over and grabbed her arm, unable to speak.

"He's going to be OK," Mari said.

The stuffing went out of her and she collapsed onto the bench. Her body was wracked with trembling. "I... thought I'd lost him," Sara said and Mari shook her head. "Thought I'd be on my own." She took hold of both Mari's hands. "Why?"

Mari looked straight at her. "That's what he saw every day," she risked saying.

"What?"

"Getting hit, being hurt..."

Sara gawped at her. "I never touched a hair on his head." This was hard for Mari to believe. "He always had some story about falling over or a fight; always something wrong with him. I didn't get it..." She paused. "You thought!" Sara's brow furrowed and she dropped Mari's hands. Mari shook her head. "You thought I could hurt him?" Sara's cheeks flushed. "I could never... *never* harm that boy."

Mari felt guilt plucking at her sleeve. "I'm sorry."

The nurse had returned. "Excuse me?" The women looked up. "You can come and see him now: one at a time."

The pair looked at each other.

"You go," Mari said.

Getting up, Sara touched Mari's shoulder. "Thank you."

Mari waited until she'd gone into the ward then stood in the doorway herself.

In the side-ward, Dafydd was lying on the bed, his arms in white bandages. The red pipes feeding him blood looked like super-long bendy straws, as at some children's party ended in disaster. Seeing him open his eyes as she approached, Sara gripped his hand and stooped to kiss him on the head. She was weeping. Dafydd opened his lips but Sara shushed him. He leaned back, drinking in his mother's new-found tenderness.

Mari felt her guts unravelling. Doctor's orders: "He'll need someone to look after him." Sara looked as though she knew at last who was son and who was mother; who was ill and who in health. Mari stayed in the doorway, peeping in. Then she turned, went out into the corridor and let the chain slough from her hand to the lino. Waiting beneath the porch as dark clouds threatened, she realised her hands were caked in dried blood. Stepping outside, Mari held up her palms to the raindrops which kindly washed off the map of iron-coloured contours.

Chapter 37

"Thank God you're back!" The nurse seemed harassed but she smiled. "She's been asking for you non-stop." Mari put the buttermilk down to sign the book. "To be honest, her antics have kept us up all hours. I thought you'd never come and we had no phone number." Mari's chest hurt. "You know the way." The nurse took a phone call.

Mari went down the corridor which looked smaller now: the way they always do second time around. She opened the door. There she was in exactly the same place. As Mari went over, Eunice didn't stir from her vigil over the garden. Mari sat down and each waited for the other to break the silence.

"It's unnatural somehow, don't you think?" the old woman asked. Mari followed her eyeline to where a butterfly was nagging a late rose.

"It's been so warm this year," Mari agreed.

Her mother's voice had weakened. "Some of them only live one day, you know? The morning sun dries their wings when they hatch and the evening sun fades them when their time's up."

Eunice's ague was worse and she was obviously in pain. The insect was blooming purple against petals of peach. Her mother's skin was desiccated, her breathing faint.

"There's one butterfly," Eunice said, "the large blue they call it... She lays her eggs near an ants' nest! *Well...*" Mari let her run on, wondering if it had been Eunice, after all, who had been the teacher in the family. "...She leaves the little ones by someone else's nest so they can bring them up." Heavens, what was her mother telling her? Eunice was still not looking at Mari, who reached for her hand and squeezed. "The ants, they're head over heels, running after each nipper like he was their own flesh and blood." Mari looked at the raggedy scrap of colour perched on a leaf outside. "They look after him, keep him clean and stroke him, even though they're chalk and cheese. They would die for him, they would!" Her eyes were watery: a tear escaped. "That's what large blues do: trick others into building nests better than they ever could." Mari looked down at their laced-together hands, then her mother caught her eye. "You had a good home, didn't you? Knowing that lets me sleep at night. That's why I chose the vicar."

Eunice scanned her daughter's face. Mari thought of every knock her ego took, each cross she'd had to bear. Playing alone on the lawn. Prayers on the slate floor. Black looks, blame, the lectures. All from a man for whom girl spelt stranger. Her mother couldn't read her thoughts.

"I had a good home," was Mari's answer.

Despite the lie, the silence between them stayed easy.

"They gave you a pretty name," Eunice said. Mari smiled and her mother went on, "I was in love with him, see? I loved your father, but I was already married. We'd married so young – I'm a real one for a chap in uniform, you know. But then back he came, my husband – back from the war, you know – and... things weren't the same... He was a different man... away with work all the time... Couldn't pin him down! I met someone else and then... But I had to give you up: do the right thing."

"You mean leaving a baby?"

"Well, yes."

In Eunice's dreams across sixty years, that speech had been playing. Sweet sixteen in a prom dress, her girl would rush into her arms and be blessed with just the right words. What she'd left out was this. Eunice had refused to leave her husband so her lover had married someone else. Her own husband, a few years down the line, had jilted her for a younger woman from work. And then depression's sponge had sat on her.

There were so many things Mari wanted to ask her, but she couldn't recall any right now. Once more her mother's eyes were lost to mist.

"I'm glad you came, dear," Eunice said, squeezing her daughter's fingers. "So glad you came."

"Why," Mari began. Eunice turned towards her. "Why did you leave that necklace on me?"

The strawberry necklace the papers had mentioned. Like a daisy chain but with real wild fruit for decoration, runners looped around the sweet tears and twisted tight around her neck. By the time she'd been found, the red dabs had softened, leaving syrupy wounds that perplexed the police.

Eunice smiled. "We'd meet by the railway line: pick them in summertime. You were such a doll! I didn't want my heart broken twice over... You'd have traced me in a jiffy if you'd had a proper chain..." It must have lasted just the one night. Yet Mari found the thought of the fruit necklace a comfort. "Nearly dinnertime," her mother said.

"Yes," Mari answered.

The butterfly went up and away across the garden like a lost leaf. Eunice turned to smile at her.

"I'd better go," Mari said, getting up.

The horizon was still of great interest to Eunice but she was shaking less. "I'm tired," she said, plucking at Mari's lapel to bring her nearer. "So very tired."

Mari bent to kiss her mother. Eunice cupped her hand around Mari's chin so that they were cheek-to-cheek, about to waltz should a band strike up. The women were so close, so long, that their tears began to mingle. It dawned on them both: so this is what life is about...

Chapter 38

Mari opened her eyes. The white of a new day was wiping the world, leaving the window a square of light. She got up, finding the house cold. The sea was a sharp slice of sapphire. She put on the clothes set ready in a neat pile beside the bed. Her skin was up in goose pimples and her breath was a snake sloughing skin against the air. Mari tugged her shoes on and found a comb in her bag to catch stray wisps. She took the suitcase out with her, leaving the door open.

From the empty chest in the best room she took the leather box and tucked it loosely into the crook of her arm. At the front door she waited with her hand on the knob, listening. The cottage was an empty shell but the sound of the sea was coming from outside. Dawn had broken a string of pearls across the lawn; they'd been caught in silk nets spun by spiders overnight. Mari gazed towards the sea. Or were they lucky glass floats cast by fishermen out to maximise their catch? The land and the sea seemed to merge into one big adventure. Mari picked up her bag and closed the door behind her. She pointed her car towards the sale.

The jewellery was sold and scattered. Every story smashed, each vow invalidated. The gemstones flirted at their new owners like professionals, tucking their tender core neatly under flounces of colour and sheen. Before going under the hammer, held up between thumb and forefinger, each had flashed their talents for all they were worth: the massive sapphire and the icy diamond, the ring she'd bought from the quiet man, and the brooches. The auctioneer held the emerald high above his head and Mari watched it work its magic on the crowd. She looked away grimly as greed spread along the benches, sending the price soaring. She went over to stand at the entrance until it was all over, then she went to collect her recompense. Outside, it was still early morning and Mari had a life of her own to lead.

Chapter 39

It was a wild winter's night, the wind sweeping waves of drizzle across the sky. On the doormat dry leaves were drifting instead of correspondence. Dai had offered to come too but Mo had insisted she work alone. It was practically empty, anyway. The chalk-stick was powdering her warm palm. With her lamp lit, Mo took a right turn into a small room with a sea view. Here, there was a toy box, a desk and a wooden chair in the window. She marked the first two out of habit and sat in the third. Were such big crosses really necessary, she thought? The house was bereft of clutter, after all. The rain was driving through the darkness outside.

Mo recalled all the houses she'd cleared with Mari, the town houses and the hovels. Families can get lost along the wayside and so the pair's service had been to the dead, helping them tie up their lives tidily. Some were less tangled than others, that's all. Mo got up and marked a cross where she'd been sitting. Places always looked so roomy without the furniture. In the little bedroom she knew so well, she ran a finger along the base of the bed. That could be sold, and the chest of drawers.

So this was the favour Mo would do Mari, in exchange for the lucky glass floats. Had she realised, Mo would never have taken them. But they'd shaken hands on it. Her eye was caught by something on the mantelpiece. Mo put her lamp down and sat on the bed to open it. Among the long shadows cast by lamplight, she imagined the bars of a cage and shivered. From its soft dark cube, a ring with a clean deep ruby shone.

Mo hooked it out. She'd never been given anything like this before. She slid it onto her finger and it was a perfect fit. It glinted at her when she held her palm facing outwards. She blinked back tears. Just as Mari had requested, she had taken the proceeds from the emerald ring to the home, to make sure Eunice could stay there indefinitely. When Mo's lamp went out, she sat in darkness, soaked in the sense of longing that had seeped into the house. But she didn't resist it. Mari had shown Mo that you shouldn't fear shadow, and that wisdom Mo would keep forever.

Lights funnelled down the road and a car stopped outside. She'd hardly managed to struggle up when she heard footsteps and the door opened.

"Mo?"

"Dai?" He came in holding a bag. They sat down together on the bed, her husband appreciating Mo's unusual silence. He grabbed her hand awkwardly.

"I've brought a snack: tea, cake."

Mo nodded and smiled through her tears, squeezing his hand tenderly.

After they'd eaten, Mo got up and gave herself a little shake. She went out to the car to fetch black bags, took up a brush and her cleaning stuff. Dai and Mo began to clear out the lonely little cottage above the sea.

Chapter 40

In the city, a young woman was washing the floor. Her knees were now clean of blood, and she'd thrown the towels into a bin bag. Having laboured for hours, she was exhausted. Sweat was pouring from her forehead and her arms were shaking. She wiped the floor one last time and went into the other room. It was midnight. A whimper came from the bed. She paced up and down, her arms loose by her side.

"Shshshsh... shshshshsh..." She had no patience: she just had to get away. She wrung her hands and the crying came again. "Shshshshsh, sweetie pie."

Among the bedclothes was his naked body in spasm. She had tried to wash him but there were yellow bits still stuck in his hair. She picked up the baby boy and wrapped him in an old coat, then got herself dressed to go out. He weighed next to nothing and his weeping was getting weaker. She pressed the button in the lift, averting her eyes from the face her hands were cupped around. She left the flats and went across the park. The neon haze seemed somehow natural. His limbs made a little crawling movement and she felt terrified. She had no family, no one she could trust. She was new to the area. Her lover had rejected her, even though he must have known she'd a baby on the way. She had to armour her heart to avoid it being pierced by those small faint squeals. He'd have a good home, a better place than she herself could give him.

Catrin walked along the street and stopped by the newsagent's. They would open early, before any other shop.

They'd be bound to find the baby. Take him to hospital. Glancing left and right, she hugged him for the last time. She laid him safe in the lee of the door. She turned her back on Dafydd's baby and pulled her coat tightly around her empty folds of flesh.

It was getting colder. As Catrin walked away, the baby's crying ceased. His brand new blue eyes were flickering open. The moon was gone but the sign flashing 'News' caught his soft pale nape in its glare. Back arched and arms outreached, the boy was fighting for his life. He looked up and the sky held him in a trance. The stars, though, were pure indifference.

Chapter 41

Gwyn had made himself at home in the revamped market which had swallowed up the old building. Shoppers were rushing by the lonely and the lost. There was so much more space on the new stand to display his dolls' houses. He'd been burning the candle at both ends to get it ready. And he'd come in first thing, before it got too busy. Putting the finishing touches to his pride, his joy, his baby.

Bundled up against the cold, the old man had carried the house from his car. Giving it prime position, Gwyn had whipped away the blanket with a conjuror's flourish and wide grin. A fanfare would have been fitting. He stuck the plug in the wall and opened up the front, fussing with its contents so that each pillow was plumped, each antimacassar perched at just the right angle. The gemstone clock was given a miniature adjustment to make time run forwards again. Its deep-timbred ticking managed an echo even around such flimsy four walls. Gwyn stood back: it was all in place. He flicked the switch, his heart going through the roof as the house lit up. It was perfect, a little world of its own, set between the keys and the sole-less shoes. The living room, bathed in yellow lamplight, was the house's human hub. In an armchair, toes curled into the hearthrug and a cat on her lap, was a woman. Gwyn stroked her thumbnail face with one tender fingertip and then he turned away. She was her spitting image, sitting in the warm. Her smile was broad. The fire was dancing and – no mistaking – Mari was home.

ABOUT HONNO

Honno Welsh Women's Press was set up in 1986 by a group of women who felt strongly that women in Wales needed wider opportunities to see their writing in print and to become involved in the publishing process. Our aim is to develop the writing talents of women in Wales, give them new and exciting opportunities to see their work published and often to give them their first 'break' as a writer. Honno is registered as a community co-operative. Any profit that Honno makes is invested in the publishing programme. Women from Wales and around the world have expressed their support for Honno. Each supporter has a vote at the Annual General Meeting. For more information and to buy our publications, please write to Honno at the address below, or visit our website: www.honno.co.uk

Honno, 14 Creative Units, Aberystwyth Arts Centre,
Aberystwyth, Ceredigion SY23 3GL

Honno Friends

We are very grateful for the support
of the Honno Friends:
Jane Aaron, Gwyneth Tyson Roberts, Beryl Thomas

For more information on how you can support Honno, see:
https://www.honno.co.uk/about/support-honno/